Hong Kong House

*Four novellas about life at 169
Boundary Street. Hong Kong.*

Marie Conyers McKay

WestBow
PRESS
A DIVISION OF THOMAS NELSON

ISBN: 978-1-4497-1936-4 (e)
ISBN: 978-1-4497-1937-1 (sc)
ISBN: 978-1-4497-1938-8 (hc)
Library of Congress Control Number: 2011912317

WestBow Press books may be ordered through booksellers or by contacting:

WestBow Press
A Division of Thomas Nelson
1663 Liberty Drive
Bloomington, IN 47403
www.westbowpress.com
1-(866) 928-1240

Printed in the United States of America

WestBow Press rev. date: 9/20/2011

Thanks to Elaine Hancock, Kathryn White, Millie Lovegren, and Jaxie Short, dedicated servants of our Lord, and willing to share their experiences to help new comers.

Thanks to other missionaries to Hong Kong, who taught me much.

Thanks to many Chinese Christians who accepted me as a co-worker, and listened to my fractured language.

And to Sam, Leighanne, Susan.

169 Boundary Street

Boundary Street follows the line across the Kowloon Peninsula that marked the land ceded to Great Britain in 1860, following the Opium War in the 1840's. The Kowloon Peninsula and Hong Kong Island gave the British a sheltered harbor. Later on, in 1898, Britain leased more, called the New Territories, for 99 years.

Boundary Street merged into Prince Edward Road near the walled city that remained Chinese territory. A small market area grew up nearby, and in 1932, Kai Tak airport was built on the nearly flat shore, the runway parallel to Lion Rock Mountain that rose above.

A building boom resulted with many apartment buildings erected along Boundary Street, all three stories, or less, due to the flight pattern of planes landing.

169 Boundary was such a building, "U" shaped; with two apartments on each floor one on each leg of the "U". The large living room was at the bottom of the "U", a beautiful room with parquet wood floors, a fire place, and opening onto a veranda with a solid banister about three feet high. A dining room, two bedrooms, breakfast nook, and a small bath finished the front of the apartment. Up a few steps, in the back were the kitchen, two small servant rooms, and a tiny bath on the back ledge.

Inside the legs of the "U" was mostly waste land. Some wells furnished water, non-potable, for flushing. Flower pots, some broken, some with dead plants were here and there.

Across the top of the legs of the "U" were small rooms used for different purposes, depending on the residents of the building.

I lived in such a building in the early 1960's. I heard stories about the police using the ground floor for a Charge Room in the early days, and the small rooms in back for holding cells. And about the Japanese that used the building when they occupied the colony, how many Chinese died in those cells. After the war it was almost impossible to rent because many feared the ghosts of those who had died there. A circus group and others had sheltered in those apartments. Finally, a mission group from the U. S. leased the whole building for $100. (US) a month. Years later the group bought the building, then in 1990's sold it to a developer after the airport was moved and the height restrictions relaxed.

I looked at the twelve-inch thick brick walls, built to withstand typhoons, at the Poinciana tree in front with its blossoms on the level of the third floor, and the "orchid" tree at the side of the driveway, and wondered what the walls would say if they could talk.

Here are some of those stories. Read and enjoy.

CONTENTS

We Go Out to Hong Kong

Chapter One

I, Joan, was ten when my father accepted a transfer to the Hong Kong Police for three years. This was in 1938. We had been living in a cold water flat in London, and Mum hated to leave. She had never been outside London before. All of her family were not far away. She had a red nose and watery eyes all the time since she cried a lot when Father told us he had accepted the transfer.

I felt confused. Father said that life would be better, that we would have servants and would live like kings. I thought about missing my friends, and that hateful Millie Jones, with her big blue eyes and her long blond hair, like a model, who had once slapped me with her raincoat belt when I wanted to walk home with her after school. I wouldn't miss her at all. But Leanna, I would miss her. Even when I teased her and called her Leanna Banana, she didn't care. She just laughed.

But the day came that we went to Southhampton to board the P and O liner *Orestus* for Hong Kong. We were all scared. We had never seen such a big boat. Father kept sitting down, taking out a cigarette, lighting it, then throwing it away, getting up, and walking around our little group, then sitting down and repeating the exercise.

It was a six-week trip, part of a round-the-world excursion for some of the passengers. We traveled in limited first class, which meant that our stateroom was down on the third deck, with a porthole for a window, the bath was on the hall, and we slept in bunk beds, all five of the family in one room. Younger than I at eight was Emma, and then the baby, Maggie, at five.

We all ate at the first sitting. Some parents sent their children to the first sitting alone, and they sometimes acted like monkeys, throwing food and running around. But my parents ate with us at the same table and made us act as we did at home, using proper manners and the right fork. I think my parents didn't know that they were allowed to let their children eat by themselves. They had never been on a ship before, either.

We were all sick the first night out as we left the English Channel and rounded the point of France into the Atlantic. We lay in our bunks, sometimes throwing up into the little bowls that Mum had brought with us. Mum had to get up and take care of us, even though she was sick herself.

When morning came, no one wanted to get up, dress, and go eat. Later, the steward knocked on the door and asked if we wanted anything.

"It will be calmer by tomorrow," he said, "and when we get down to the Mediterranean, you will think we are in a lake, it will be so quiet."

Father decided to get up and go to the topside deck to see what the ocean was like. I wanted to go with him. But I couldn't stand up; my head was so dizzy. I lay back down on my bunk quickly.

"Never mind, pet," Father said. "Maybe you will feel better later."

When he came back, his brown hair was windblown and his face ruddy.

"Truly bracing, the cold wind." He drew a deep breath. "They say you will feel better faster in the fresh air. Do any of you want to try it?"

No one answered.

By the next morning, we had recovered. The ship had passed into calmer waters, and we could stand, dress, and walk without mishap.

We went to breakfast, ate everything on the plates, and then went out on deck. That began a long period of warm, sunlit, happy days for us on that ship. We ate well, we walked on the deck, we played games, and we even swam in the saltwater pool. The pool scared me. When the water shifted with the rise and fall of the ship, sometimes the two-foot end would suddenly become six feet deep. So I stayed in the kiddie pool with my sisters.

We came to Gibraltar and went ashore to see the Barbary apes. I enjoyed seeing our soldiers in uniform on guard, and I felt that I wasn't so far from home after all. We could see Morocco on the right across the water. Mum was determined that this would be an educational trip for us. One ape put his hand in the pocket of my dress and pulled out my handkerchief. I never got it back. And that night I discovered that I had flea bites all over my legs. They itched like mad.

Then to Malta and on to the Suez Canal. It began to be hot as we made our way through the narrow strip of water that made the trip so much shorter. Everywhere we stopped was a British territory. I've heard it said that the sun never sets on the British Empire.

Then on to India. Father had police friends in Delhi and had written ahead to ask that they show us some of the city in the three days we would be there.

We stayed one night at the house of the friends in Delhi. That was my first experience with an amah, or any servants in the house. I saw how life was much easier with an amah to do the work. The daughter my age did nothing in her room. The amah made the bed, picked up the clothes, even helped her dress and tied her shoes. She would have helped me, too, but I can take care of myself now that I'm a big girl. She did help Maggie, and Emma asked her to brush her long, curly, auburn hair. I can comb my carrot-colored, straight hair myself. Maggie had reddish-blond wavy hair, and I often help her comb it.

We stopped again in Singapore before we got to Hong Kong, and there we said "God bless" to several families that were on the ship as they transferred to another ship to Australia or stayed in Malaya. We went to the Raffles Hotel for tea to please Mum. We three girls wore our hats and gloves and were as quiet as mice in the elegant place with white-jacketed waiters. The flowers outside and in made the air smell like a perfume shop.

We got up early on the day we arrived in Hong Kong Harbor. The sun was just breaking through the fog as the ship came through the eastern channel. The island was on our left, with buildings on the waterfront and up the side of the mountain. On the right was the mainland, with a train terminal and a tall clock on the shore.

I looked over the side of the ship and watched the little boats pushed by long poles skim the water. They looked like bugs; they were so small compared with the ship I was on.

"Where is Maggie?" Mum called out. We looked around and couldn't see her. "Joan, go see if you can find her."

I hated to leave my good place at the rail. I frowned as I looked around for Maggie. I really love Maggie, but she is an aggravation. I walked back toward the steps that went down to our cabin. There, playing with Albert, a little boy who was also going to Hong Kong, was Maggie. I took her by the hand and pulled her with me to Mum. By that time Maggie was crying, and Mum scolded me for making Maggie cry.

The ship moved slowly through the harbor, the little boats scrambling to get out of the way. We moved to the right side of the harbor, with a tug pushing the ship up against the long wooden dock. The gangway was let down, but we couldn't leave until our passports had been checked. That didn't take long, as British passports are always on the top of the pile, of course.

A tall man with thinning hair and in a police uniform came on board and spoke to Father. "Evans? Good to see you. Harrison here. Welcome to Hong Kong and the police force."

He nodded to Mum, and went on talking to Father. Then he turned to Mum. "My wife will see you this afternoon and help you find your way around, get some amahs, tell you about schools, and so forth. Now, if all are ready, we will leave the ship and go to police headquarters, then on to your flat."

Chapter Two

That afternoon, we were driven to 169 Boundary Street, where our flat would be on the second floor over the police station. We were actually on the 167 side of the building on the top floor. The flat looked empty; it was so much larger than our flat in London. The police furnished beds, table and chairs, a couch, and a chair for the living room, and a gas stove in the kitchen. We had brought some small things in our freight, but would have other furniture made here. The living room and each bedroom had ceiling fans.

Our luggage was brought upstairs, and we began to unpack. We would stay tonight in our own flat. I walked out from the living room onto the veranda and looked at the red blossoms in the top of a tree in the garden. The sun was hot, and the sky was clear blue. It was September, and still hotter than July or August at home.

Down below, I could see cars, double-decker buses, and several sorts of two-wheeled carts pulled by men with people riding in them—later I found they were called rickshaws—on the two streets that ran in front of the police station.

Those two streets looked odd. In front of the police station was Boundary Street, then a small stretch of grass and another street going in the same direction. On the left in the distance, I could see that the two streets came together and formed one wide street. I was glad we were high enough that the dust and dirt from the street didn't come in the open windows.

Emma called me to go exploring with her. We walked down the hall, past the bathroom, up two steps, and turned right into the pantry. There was a built-in cabinet for dishes and an electric icebox. An open door went into the kitchen. A big iron sink was under the window, and a gas stove with an oven was across the room. The smell of cleaner was strong in the kitchen.

Out in the small back hall, tiled with black and white squares, as the kitchen was, we saw two tiny rooms, with a board on top of two sawhorses in each. Later I found that the boards were the beds. Servants' rooms, I guessed.

Emma went out the door at the end of the hall. "Come see, Joan. There's a W.C. out here."

I stepped out on the narrow walklike porch, with three strands of barbed wire stretched above the low brick wall. From here we could look down on the garages and the end of the jail cells behind our building. I looked in the open door of the W. C. and saw a shower and a toilet.

Voices came from below, but I couldn't understand them. I guess they were speaking Chinese.

Then Mum called us to come to the living room. Another lady was standing in the hall, just inside the front door.

"Girls, this is Mrs. Harrison. She will tell us about your school and other things."

We sat in the living room as Mrs. Harrison told us about Kowloon Junior School, where Maggie would be in Infants Two, Emma in Primary Two, and I in Primary Four. She would take us to the school tomorrow. Her children had gone to that school until they were old enough to send home to finish their education. I wondered what school would be like and whether I would make new friends. Suddenly, my heart felt hollow, missing my friends from home.

"Oh, you must not drink water from the tap!" Mrs. Harrison said. "All your drinking water must be boiled, even for brushing teeth. There will be water in the tap from 7:00 a.m. to 10:00 a.m., then from 4:00 to 6:00 p.m. Because there is time when there is no water in the pipes, germs grow, so all drinking water must be boiled. That will be one of the cook's main jobs."

I didn't tell her that I had tried to get a drink out of the tap already.

Her amah had recommended a couple of friends to work for us, and they would come within the hour for an interview. Mrs. Harrison spoke some Chinese, so she would help with the interview.

We unwillingly sat in the adjoining dining room with the double doors open while Mum and Mrs. Harrison interviewed the Chinese women. They had brought along another friend who spoke some English. So everything said was translated back and forth. Mum decided to hire them. The older woman would be the cook. She had cooked for foreigners before, she said. The younger woman would be the washerwoman and would clean the bedrooms and bath. The cook would clean the other rooms of the house. Since we girls could take care of ourselves, we would not hire a baby amah. I wondered what it would be like to have someone other than Mum in the kitchen. Would she make treats for us like Mum did?

We were invited to the Harrisons for dinner that night. They lived two floors below, on the ground floor. Maggie fell asleep at the table and Emma and I were struggling to keep our eyes open, so we left soon after the meal was over. I don't remember what we ate that night, but it was served by a short, Chinese woman with a long black braid down her back, wearing black pants and a white, starched, high-collared top.

We began school the next day. Within a week, we felt used to it and began to make friends. Several children from the other four police families in the building also went to Kowloon Junior, so one amah took all the children on the bus to school. Then she would meet us at the school when classes were over and bring us home.

One little boy Maggie's age kept hitting her. I tried to stop him, but then he began hitting me. We were always taught not to hit back, but to call our parents.

"If Nigel hits you first without you doing anything to him, then you may hit him back," Father told us after several days of hitting.

That night, Nigel's father came to see Father.

"Nigel says you told your girls that they could hit him. He's quite frightened," he said.

"Yes, I told them that if Nigel kept hitting them, they could hit back."

"He's hitting girls?" Nigel's father sounded surprised. "I'll talk to him about this."

That ended Nigel's hitting Maggie. They later became good friends.

9

In the school, besides the British children, were several Eurasians, two or three from India, but no Chinese. I asked Winnie, my new best friend, about it.

"Of course not; they can't go to school with us," she said.

"Why not?"

"They are not allowed."

"Why not?" I asked again.

"I don't know, but just like they are not allowed to live on the top of Victoria Peak on the Hong Kong side, they just aren't allowed."

This puzzled me. Were Chinese stupid or something?

Both my parents had language lessons, Father for his work and Mum to be able to talk to the amahs in the house. Mum took to the language better than Father, but then she had to see about food for us to eat.

Once when she had asked the cook to make muffins, that was all that was put on the table for dinner that night. Father said, "Tell the cook that man does not live by bread alone."

The cook could not read or write even Chinese. My mother took accounts with her every day, so she wouldn't forget what she had bought in the market and how much it cost. The washerwoman could read some and knew numbers, so she helped the cook sometimes.

One Saturday when Father was off, the family went to Hong Kong Island, across the harbor from where we lived. We rode the bus south to the point of the peninsula of Kowloon and took a big ferry, named the *Morning Star*, for the ten-minute ride across the water. The ferry terminal was near the dock where our ship had tied up on our arrival. We rode first class, on the top deck. Chinese ride second class, on the bottom deck.

Both end sections were enclosed, with windows that may be opened. The long middle section of the deck was open, but had canvases that could be lowered during storms. The long seats had backs that could be moved so that the bench faces either way. The ferry does not turn around; the captain just walks to the helm on the other end and drives it back.

Emma and I wanted to walk around and explore, but the boat was moving up and down so much even while loading that we were afraid we would be sick again, as we were on the *Orestus* when we came to Hong

Kong. So we sat very still. The water was calmer in the middle of the harbor, so we felt better and began to look around.

The wind blew the water into little white peaks that splashed against the ferry. It ruffled our hair as we sat in the open middle of the deck. Father pointed out things to see. There were cars and trucks on the slow, vehicular ferry off to the west. The harbor was busy with little boats called sampans, and some larger boats called junks. British Navy ships were tied up to the Admiralty docks on the Island side.

After we got off the ferry, we walked up the hill to the peak tram station, then took the tram to the top of Victoria Peak, where only British people could live. It was cool and pleasant that morning.

"The peak is often covered in fog early in the morning, I hear, and mold and mildew are problems, but it is the only cool place in the summer," Father said.

Chapter Three

Father told us some about his work each evening at dinner. His work was sometimes different from what it was in London, but sometimes almost the same. He had to have someone translate for him, but he liked being a policeman in Hong Kong.

One night he told us that as he went into the Charge Room that morning, the telephone rang with the news that there was a fire in the walled city. He explained that Hong Kong police could not go inside, because of an agreement with the Chinese government at the time Hong Kong was ceded to us.

"But the police are responsible for crowd control outside the walled city. I went with the Inspector east on Boundary Street to the shops that are just outside the walled city. The Chinese sergeant went with us."

The St. Johns' Brigade ambulance was called and came after some time to carry the injured to the new Kowloon Hospital.

"How did the fire start?" my mother asked.

"The early mornings and late evenings are very cool now, and some people light their charcoal burners, others crowd around, and the burner sometimes gets knocked over and a fire starts. These Chinks live in close quarters, so when one place burns, they all burn. Or maybe some opium addict dropped a coal when lighting his pipe."

"Which reminds me," Mother said. "We will need to buy some wood for the fireplace. That's the only heat we will have this winter. I saw some bundles of wood at the market yesterday when I went with the cook. The market is messy and wet underfoot, but much cheaper, as well as closer than the Dairy Farm store on Nathan Road, so the cook can go to the market herself," Mum said.

I liked 'A Laan, the younger amah, who washed our clothes and cleaned our bedrooms. She smiled and tried to talk to us, but her English was weird. Her black hair was cut short and permed, her face round and pretty. She called us all "Missy" for a while, then began to say, "Missy Joan" or Missy Emma" or "Missy Maggie."

We three girls shared a bedroom, and we soon let 'A Laan make the beds and pick up our dirty clothes, just like the girl in Delhi who I thought was such a baby.

The cook was older, with her hair in a thick braid, and sort of grouchy; she didn't want us in the kitchen in her way. We were used to going to the kitchen for a snack when we got home from school, but the cook wanted to bring a snack out to the breakfast nook for us. That was okay.

"Father, where can we build a bonfire for Guy Fawkes Day?" In our old neighborhood, the fathers built a fire in a vacant lot nearby.

"I don't know." He was surprised, as if he'd forgotten about it. "I'll ask the Inspector what the custom is here."

The next evening he asked, "What about a sausage sizzle up on the roof for Guy Fawkes Day?"

"Is that allowed?" I asked.

"Yes, not a bonfire, but a charcoal burner to grill the sausages. There's a sort of pavilion up there on the front part of the roof. We could invite all the children in the building, and you could dress up in costumes, if you want to."

Each child's costume was the topic of conversation on our trips back and forth to school every day. One or two knew immediately what their costume would be, but we three changed our minds every day. Emma wanted to be Shirley Temple, and Maggie thought that she should be Shirley Temple. Nigel, now in our good graces, wanted to be one of the Little Rascals kids.

We planned it for the Saturday night before November 5. It rained that morning, but cleared off in the afternoon. It turned colder as night approached. The light wind was sharp and smelled of snow somewhere in the far north. The smells and grit of the street were left down there. It was a different atmosphere on the roof.

The charcoal grill was set up on the pavilion. Under the pavilion, tiles made a smooth floor, covering the rough cement that was the top of the building.

My mother had brought a tub filled with water, and we bobbed for the apples that she floated on the water. We played some other games and marched in a parade to show off our costumes. Maggie got to be Shirley Temple, and Emma was Deanna Durban. I was a princess.

By then the sausages were done, and we ate our fill. Then we sat on the floor and sang songs. One of the fathers had bought a few fireworks, including some Roman candles, and they shot them off there on the roof.

"Who is that on the far end of the roof beyond the clothes lines?" I asked.

Father glanced over there and said, "I think the servants enjoyed seeing the fireworks; even the Chinese sergeant and his family watched."

I sighed in happiness when we went to bed. Even though life here was different, we could still have fun.

At Christ Church on Waterloo Road where we went every Sunday, we were beginning practice on a Christmas program. The children were to do a tableau of the manger scene while the choir sang. This was a new church, begun just the year before, and the building wasn't complete. We worshiped in a plain room with folding chairs, the choir on the same level as the people.

The Cathedral on the Hong Kong side was wonderful to see with the lofty roof beams showing. It was built nearly a hundred years before, just after Hong Kong became a British Crown Colony. But it was so far away from us, across the harbor and then several blocks up Garden Road. Even though the Christ Church building was nothing much to look at, we liked it.

All the children at church had a part in the tableau. Because I was tall, I was to be a wise man, Emma an angel, and Maggie a sheep. Mum was busy cutting and sewing, making our costumes.

I think it was at the first practice that I noticed the Chinese sergeant's wife and little girl, about four years old, just a year younger than Maggie.

"Phoebe, you will be a sheep, like Maggie and Nigel," the woman who was leading the tableau said.

"But she is Chinese!" Nigel said.

"Her parents are Christians, they speak English, and they come often to this church. Phoebe can be in the tableau if she wants to be."

We practiced several times, and Phoebe was present at every one. Her costume was already finished, and she wore it to a practice. We all wanted to see it and look closely at it. My mother said it must be tailor-made, it was so well done. How could they afford to have a costume tailor-made? Her father made less money than my father did, I'm sure. And Mum said we couldn't afford to have a tailor make our costumes.

The night we presented the tableau was the Sunday night before Christmas. We all crowded into the Parish Hall, which is where we have our worship until our building was finished. Many fathers smoked, and the air was thick and cloudy with it. The tree had new electric lights and sparkled in its corner. I loved the smell and sights of Christmas. I thought of the Christmases in London and longed for snow.

Before the tableau, the children stood on steps made of boards on blocks of wood and sang some Christmas songs. Nigel was so excited, and as we stepped off the boards, he jumped on the end of the bottom step, and the board flew up and hit him on the side of his head. He was bleeding and almost dead, I thought. Someone screamed, and just as suddenly, it was quiet, and I held my breath.

Nigel's parents and others ran up to the steps, pulled Nigel out from under the board, and tried to stop the spurts of blood. My father knew First Aid which all policemen had to learn in London, so he pressed the places to make the bleeding stop. Then Nigel's father carried him out of the Hall, and took him to the hospital, they said.

After things were cleaned and straightened up, we went on with the tableau as the choir sang. The children were all hushed, but did their parts without a mistake. Phoebe and Maggie made up for Nigel not being there with their loud "Babaa-baas."

"Nigel lost a lot of blood and will need a transfusion," Father told us the next day. But he had a rare type of blood, type B, and they were looking for someone with that type.

Chapter Four

"How will they find someone with Nigel's type blood?" I asked Father as we sat at the dinner table that night. We could look over the courtyard and the roof of the cells in back from the big dining-room window. Darkness had fallen, and the lights in the buildings beyond the back wall were shining.

"They will ask all the police, and the hospital may know about some people with rare blood types. They will also make radio announcements on Redifusion and the Blue Network and put it in the newspapers."

We worried all the next day. Maggie kept asking if Nigel was going to die, and I kept saying, "Of course not."

We went to school, but I couldn't keep my mind on multiplication tables and cursive writing. I felt that I was up in the air above the stuff on my desk, watching someone else do it.

As we Boundary Street kids met the amah after school, she told us that a blood donor had been found. One of the sixth-class children understood Cantonese and translated for us. It was the Sergeant in our building! He had already gone to the hospital and given the blood, and Nigel was much improved.

That night I asked Father how come it was the Chinese sergeant that matched Nigel's blood. Would that make Nigel Chinese when he grew up? Would his eyes change shape? I sat on the arm of Father's chair, and he put down his paper.

"It's a long story," Father said. "Nigel's father died before Nigel was born. Nigel's mother married again, and this husband adopted Nigel and gave him his name. So that is why both of his parents had a different blood type from him. Most Chinese in this area have type A, but the sergeant's family came from North China many years ago, so they are somewhat different from the Cantonese. You remember that the sergeant is tall for a Chinese. He says that most Northerners are taller than South Chinese are, and their faces are shaped differently. So it is not surprising that they have a different blood type. But a little Chinese blood will not make Nigel Chinese."

"Does that mean that blood is blood, whether it is British or Chinese?" I asked. "Is Chinese blood red like ours?"

"Yes, it is," he answered.

"Will Father Christmas find us in Hong Kong?" Maggie asked often. Even the tableau at church didn't reassure her that our Christmas would be the same, though there would be no snow. The day before Christmas, Father brought the tree up to our flat. We girls helped to decorate it that night. We sang carols as we always had at home. And during the night, Father Christmas found us with more toys than ever before. I was beginning to feel at home in Hong Kong and to forget about how it was back in London, although I still compared to the way things were there.

Soon after we arrived in Hong Kong in October, the Japanese took Canton, only eighty miles northwest of Hong Kong. The *South China Morning Post* had black headlines two inches high. They wondered if the Japanese would destroy Canton as they had Nanking the year before. The soldiers had done terrible things to the people in Nanking, they said.

But we weren't worried. No one would dare to attack a British colony, even one as far away from home as Hong Kong was. We weren't bothering them; why should they bother us?

Rumors about Germany getting strong again and destroying the balance of power in Europe bothered my parents more. Sometimes I heard them talking about Hitler and what he was doing in Europe. When we went to the movies, they would clack their tongues, "Tsk, tsk," over the newsreels. And they would skip over the big headlines and go to the stories about England and Europe every time. When Austria and Czechoslovakia became part of Germany, they were sad and worried.

I became aware of this because in my class at school, we had begun a unit on current events. Once a week, we had to bring a clipping from the newspaper to class and tell about it. Then we would discuss the meaning of the event for Hong Kong.

"Did you know that Canton is only eighty miles away? And did you know how fast the Japanese army can move?" I asked one night at dinner.

"Yes, Canton is only eighty miles away, but the Japanese are only interested in China. They aren't going to attack Hong Kong; you don't need to worry," Father said as he cut the meat and served our plates.

One morning 'A Laan was red-eyed and sad-looking when she came into our bedroom to help us get ready for school and pick up the dirty clothes.

"What's the matter?" I asked her as I brushed my straight hair. She picked up the brush and began on Emma's curls.

"Big brother dead," she answered.

"Your brother is dead. That's too bad. Where did he live?"

That was more than she could manage in English. Later, Mum asked Mrs. Harrison to talk to 'A Laan and find out what the situation was.

"Her brother was a soldier in the Chinese army fighting the Japanese near Canton. He was killed at that time, but word has just reached her about his death. A cousin came from Canton and brought the news to her husband's parents, and they sent someone here yesterday and told her," she told us after speaking to 'A Laan.

"Husband! We didn't know that she was married. Does she have children?" Mum asked.

"Yes, she has two children. Her husband is dead. His family keeps the children during the week, but she goes home to a village in the New Territories on Sunday, her off day," Mrs. Harrison said.

I thought of 'A Laan in a different way after that. She had a family; she missed her brother. She was a person who felt sad, just as British people did.

That night after I went to bed, I thought about 'A Laan and her dead brother. I remembered a little friend who had died two years before. She had been in an accident when a drunk driver had hit their car. Our class at school had gone to her funeral as a group. It was hard to understand why God let children be killed by someone drunk. The grown-ups spoke in hushed voices about the waste of life, as if nothing could be done. I remembered how solemn the funeral was and how I missed my friend at school. Would I die like that? Or my sisters? 'A Laan's brother had died.

Finally, I drew a long breath and prayed the night prayer again: "Now I lay me down to sleep …" I was asleep before I finished it.

I read the newspaper every day now, after school but before Father got home. I found it in the living room, on the chair where Father always sat. It was already dark outside the windows onto the veranda, and I could see the lights on the streets below. Sometimes the fire still burned in the fireplace and would be built up just before Father came. It was nice to sit by the fire and read.

"Who is Chamberlain that the paper talks about every day?" I asked.

"He is the Prime Minister, silly," Emma said, . "Even I know that."

"He says that even though Japan has signed an agreement with Germany and now Italy to resist communism, they will not attack the UK nor any part of the Empire. He says we can give Germany what it wants and they will leave us alone."

"I hope so. They won't dare to attack us, I'm sure. You girls don't need to worry about Hitler," Mum said as she came in the dining room bringing the soup for dinner. The double doors from the living room into the dining room were open.

We listened to the BBC news on the new shortwave radio that Father bought. I could tell that my parents were worried about war in Europe. I guess they talked about it after we had gone to bed. Sometimes, I heard them before I went to sleep. My grandparents, aunts, and uncles were in London. If Hitler attacked England, London would be the first target. What would we do?

Easter was the end of March that year, 1939. We had new outfits for church that Sunday, with hats and gloves and little purses. Maggie immediately lost her gloves and cried all the way to church in the taxi.

"Never mind, Maggie. It will soon be too hot to wear gloves anyway," I said as I tucked my gloves in my purse. I felt grown-up in the new dress, my first to have bust darts. I wore long silk stockings and white slippers—no baby straps for me now.

That Sunday afternoon we went to the Botanical Gardens, near Government House on the Hong Kong side. The azaleas were in bloom, with red and orange blossoms mixed together.

"Why don't they move the plants so that all the reds are together and all the orange together in another place? I don't like to see colors mixed that way. It hurts my eyes and makes me feel sick," I said.

Father looked at me, then said, "I thought after we looked at the flowers, we would stop at the fish-and-chips place down by the Star Ferry. Will your tummy feel better so that you can eat?"

He was teasing me. He knew that I could always eat fish-and-chips.

Chapter Five

We had our first typhoon in early June. The weather became warm and muggy. Mum thought it must mean a storm coming. But she never expected that the storm would be so severe. In London, we had wind and rain and sometimes snow, but never a storm like this typhoon.

The number eight typhoon ball was raised early one morning. That meant that the center of the typhoon was less than twelve hours away from Hong Kong. We listened to the radio for instructions. The number eight ball meant that we did not go to school, all businesses were closed, and the ferries to the Hong Kong side had been stopped. We stayed in all day. Father, of course, had to go to work.

"There was not much to do today, except in the late afternoon we were called to go out to the airport," Father said at dinner that night. "A BOAC plane had to land because of a petrol shortage, and as it turned out, the plane was blown off the runway. People were in the ocean, but we got most of them out and to the terminal building. The runway is on the level land near the shore, so there is no protection from the waves blown high by the wind. I had taken the Chinese sergeant and several patrolmen. They were courageous and the Sergeant smart. He spaced them and tied them together with rope then passed the passengers up the rope to safety. We were able to rescue most of them."

"Some were hurt?" Mum asked as we all sat wide-eyed at the story, forgetting to eat our dinner.

"A few. But some were already dead when we got them out of the water."

"I heard on the radio that the winds are about 150 miles per hour," I said as I passed the rolls to Maggie.

"Yes, and they are stronger now. Sometime tonight, the eye will pass over Hong Kong; then the wind will come from a different direction," he said.

"Will our building stand against such a strong wind?" Mum asked.

My stomach tightened and my hands shook at the idea of the building blowing down.

"Oh, yes. The walls are built twelve inches thick with bricks. Everything built in Hong Kong now must be able to withstand typhoons," he said. "And all the electric and telephone lines are now put underground, so we can rest easy tonight."

The wind howled, and the rain hit against the windows. I wondered if the glass would break, but then went to sleep, confident that we were safe. The next morning, all was quiet, and a weak sun shone through the lingering clouds. We saw limbs, leaves, and other debris in the streets as we went to school, but the air smelled clean and sweet; all the dirt and fumes from the city had been blown away.

The teacher always read a Psalm to begin the day. That day she said, "There were many people who live on small boats in the harbor, and some that live in shacks on the hillsides, that were swept away by the storm. The wind and high tides made a wave that nothing could stand against. Even a freighter was blown onto the railroad tracks in the New Territories, as if it were going to Canton by land. We must be thankful for our safety during the storm."

I shivered at the thought of being washed away in a big wave. We had not yet learned to swim. Perhaps we would during school holidays.

We were out of school from mid-July to the beginning of September. We went to Cheung Chau for four days near the end of July. Many foreigners who lived and worked in China came to Cheung Chau for holidays in the summer, Mrs. Harrison had told my mother. Many still worked in China, even though the Japanese controlled much of the country. There might be some vacationing on Cheung Chau now. The police had a flat that officers and families could use for a few days. Father signed up early for the four days.

I packed and unpacked my wicker suitcase several times. Mum checked it each time and made suggestions. Emma knew exactly what she wanted to take, and when Mum had okayed it, she was finished. But I couldn't make up my mind. Should I take my new Easter dress and shoes? Mum thought not. She took us shopping one day, and we got new play clothes for all three of us.

Mum packed for Maggie, and finally, the night before we were to leave, we were ready. 'A Laan would go with us to help keep an eye on Maggie and do the food shopping. My mother would cook.

We left Boundary Street early one morning, catching a bus on Prince Edward Road that would take us to the Star Ferry. On the Hong Kong side, we took a taxi to the outlying islands ferry pier. It was near enough that we could walk, but with the luggage, Father thought we should take a taxi. The morning air was cool but the sun was warm, so the day would heat up and the slightly fishy smell would become stronger.

This ferry was smaller than the Star Ferries, but looked almost the same. We, of course, rode first class. 'A Laan rode downstairs in second class. The ride was about an hour, and I enjoyed watching the other passengers. Some were eating their breakfasts that they had brought with them in covered pails. Others were reading the newspaper, and some were sleeping.

When I got tired of people watching, I looked at the water as it broke across the front of the ferry and went off in small waves on each side. We met a ferry coming in from Cheung Chau or Silvermine Bay on Laantau Island, or maybe both. The upper deck on that boat was almost full, while ours was half empty.

"When we get to Cheung Chau, we will walk to the police flat. No cars or buses are allowed on the island. We will hire a man with a cart to help with the luggage," Father said.

He pointed out the two rounded ends of the island, with small peaks on them, and the narrow strip of land that connected the two ends. Some people call it the "Dumbbell Island" because of its shape.

Maggie had gone down stairs to be with 'A Laan, and Mum called down to Maggie to stay with 'A Laan until we got ashore. As they got off the lower deck, a British policeman stopped 'A Laan, asking where she was going with the British child.

"It's okay, officer. This is my child, and this is our amah, who takes care of us." Father hurried up to them. Maggie was crying, frightened by the officer.

The policeman smiled, then said, "With the Japanese advancing in China, there have been several kidnappings to make money. So we have to be careful."

Father picked Maggie up, and she soon stopped crying as we walked to the flat. I wondered if someone would try to kidnap me. I was glad the man with the cart full of luggage followed close behind. I didn't want to lose my luggage, either.

One day we went to East Beach; the next we went to West Beach. We explored the pirates' cave and climbed the peak at one end of the island. We saw the tall, conical racks where the buns were mounted during the Bun Festival in May each year. I had seen the pictures of the festival in the newspaper.

I especially liked the beach, playing in the sand. But my sisters and I didn't learn to swim. "Joan, you'll need lessons at the 'Y' to learn to swim. I'll investigate when we get back home," Mum said.

During August we went every day for three weeks for swimming lessons at the "Y." Emma and I could swim well by the end of that time. Maggie had cried with fear every day. By the end of the three weeks, she was no longer afraid of the water, but couldn't swim yet.

"Next year we will join the Athletic Club. They have a lovely pool and tennis courts, as well as a lawn bowling court. Then you can swim every day, if you wish," Father said.

School had barely started when England declared war on Germany after they invaded Poland. The Prime Minister sounded sad as he read the declaration on the radio. Mum's younger brother had joined up, and other relatives, too. Every letter from home brought more worrisome news. I heard my parents talking quietly when we were in bed, about Germany taking over Austria and Czechoslovakia.

Mum was crying one day when we got home from school. "Some of the distant cousins decided to send their children to Canada because of the threat of war in Europe. They went by boat, and a German U-boat sank it and they all died."

I remembered our trip out from home and how much fun we had on the ship after we got used to the motion. And the plane had gone off the runway, so it wasn't safe to travel by ship or plane. I was glad we were safe here in Hong Kong and not going anywhere.

"The Japanese Army has moved a little closer to Hong Kong. They seem to want to pretend they will attack us. But if they invade, the main force will come by sea, we are sure. The army has gun emplacements on the hills facing out to sea. They will protect Hong Kong from any invasion," Father said one evening as we ate.

"But will the Japanese attack Hong Kong?" I asked. "What would we do?"

"I really don't think they will. We still are a great power in the world, much greater than Japan. They will think twice before attacking a colony of Great Britain," Father reassured us.

He could see by our faces that the idea frightened us. Where would we go? Hong Kong was a small colony, and a long way from another British outpost. If the Japanese did attack, could help come in time? I drew a long breath and suddenly wasn't hungry anymore.

Chapter Six

In October, our class began to plan for a field trip to the bird sanctuary at Mirs Bay. Two classes, Primary Five and Six, were going. Our permission slips were in to the teachers, and we had pictures of the birds so we could identify the birds we would see. One area of the coast at Mirs Bay was marshy, and many kinds of birds landed there on their trip from Siberia to warm climates.

This was my first field trip. Maggie had gone to see the Freezin' Hot Thermos Company last year, and Emma had gone to the Marine Police Headquarters and seen the typhoon warning balls in storage waiting to be hoisted during a storm. But my class trip was before we arrived in late September last year.

"Tomorrow when you come to school, bring your water bottle and your lunch in a sack," my teacher said. "Wear sturdy shoes and suitable clothes, not your uniforms. We will hike from the road down to the shore, watch the birds, eat our lunch, and hike back to the road, where the bus will be waiting for us. Are there any questions?"

"So, you are going on a field trip tomorrow, Joan," Father said at dinner that night. "Where are you going?"

"Mirs Bay to watch the birds," I said.

"Mirs Bay?" Alarm sounded in his voice, and he stopped serving the plates. "Please be careful. I was there not long ago, and some of the areas off the path have quicksand in them. You might be swallowed up. So stay on the path!"

Then I saw the glint in his eyes. He was teasing me. I laughed. "Okay, I'll stay on the path," I said.

"Mum, may I wear the new pink neck scarf? It'll be a cool morning."

"Oh, yes, I guess so."

October is one of the nicest months in Hong Kong. The humidity has dropped and the rains have stopped, but the sun is still warm in the middle of the day. Mornings and evenings are cooler, and everyone feels better.

The next morning, we went to our classroom, then out to the bus. The school had rented two ordinary city buses for our trip. The sun shone brightly, but the air was cool.

"Joan! Joan! Over here!" My friend Winnie had found an empty seat.

"Ouch!" Someone pulled my hair! I was letting it grow out to have pigtails instead of the "shingled up the back, fringe in front" that I had always worn. I turned around and stared at Billy West. He sat there looking innocent. But I knew he was guilty.

The buses started rolling down the street, and we were on our way. Our sweaters were soon too warm. Winnie pulled hers off and stuffed it in her bag. I did the same, but kept the pretty pink scarf on and stroked it. It was made of Celanese, a new, silky cloth. The boys pulled down the window by their seat, and the wind blew our hair. I tied the scarf around my neck and let the ends blow free, like aviators in the Great War. I felt so good. This was the most fun I'd had. I forgot about the war in Europe and the Japanese in China. We were safe and happy.

We drove out Castle Peak Road, past the dye yards with their big, bright-colored skeins of yarns laid out drying, around the end of Lion Rock Mountain, and past the Amah Rock. Winnie told me the story of the amah whose husband went into China to fight in a war and never came back. She stood looking for him with her baby on her back until she turned into rock.

Then we went through a little fishing village, Sha Tin, where the train tracks lie crowded between the road and the mountainside. Just before we got to Tai Po Market, the buses turned off the blacktop onto a graveled road. The dust from the bus in front came in the open window, and soon we were all covered with it.

After a while, the buses stopped, and we began to pile out. Each class stayed with their own teacher, and we walked down the paths to the shore.

On each side of the path were rocks, and some straggly grass and brush. Farther off the paths were the patches of marshy ground, with the still-green grass growing tall.

On the shore, we stood looking at the sky, a clear blue but with thin clouds here and there. The teacher told us all to be quiet, so as not to scare the birds.

"Look," my teacher said quietly, and pointed to the big bird that landed on the shore to our right. "That is a black stork, I do believe." She got out her book of birds. "Yes, it is. See here." She passed the book to let us see the picture.

Other birds, large and small, landed nearby. But when we made noise, they would suddenly whoosh away, a whole flock of them at one time.

After watching for a while, Winnie and I found a dry place to sit and ate our lunches. I was glad for the water bottle I carried in a harness over my chest. My throat was dry as the dust on the road.

"Fire! Fire!" I heard children in the other class yelling. I looked to see if I could see the fire. I stood up and walked a few feet around a rock to see what was burning.

"Joan, Joan, come back," Winnie called to me.

Suddenly, the fire was all around me. Where had it come from?

Men wearing uniforms of the marine police came running to where we were. They rushed the class up the trail back to the buses.

One of the policemen took hold of my arm, but the scarf around my neck was on fire. He pulled on the scarf, but it was knotted. I was frantic to get it off, as the flames ran up the scarf. Then the ends of my hair were on fire. He used a knife to cut the scarf, then beat out my hair with his hands, but some of the Celanese stuck to my skin. My neck felt like it was still burning, and I was crying. Through my tears, I saw the policeman's hands were burned, and he grimaced in pain.

Another policeman ran to their boat and found the first-aid kit. He pulled out the tube of Unguentine as he ran back, and he began applying it to my neck and the policeman's hands; then he wrapped gauze bandages around the burns.

The police took me and the burned policeman on their boat to go to the hospital. "It's a good thing we knew about your field trip and made arrangements to check on you. Taking you back on the boat is much quicker than the bus on the road; there is also no dust to infect the burns. We have made arrangements with your teacher. We will radio your parents to meet us at the hospital," they told me.

"O-oh," I was still crying and moaning. My neck hurt and felt like the fire was still burning. Then one of them came with a needle and gave me a shot, and I went to sleep.

I awoke at the hospital with Mum standing over me. Father was standing next to her.

"She's awake," Mum said. "Joan, honey, how do you feel?"

"My neck hurts. The pink scarf burned up. Did the other kids get home okay?"

I don't remember much for several days, except that my neck still hurt.

One day, the policeman with the burned hands came to see me. "How are you?" he said in broken English.

"How are your hands?" I asked.

"Not good; fingers stiff. But doctor say can operate."

I asked the Sister the next day about his hands. "The burns from the Celanese scarf were severe. It doesn't burn like natural fabrics, but sticks to the skin. The burns made his fingers stiff in a curved position, but he is lucky. At this time, a famous reconstructive hand surgeon is here in the colony. He is a missionary with the Church Missionary Society in India and does surgery on hands stiffened by leprosy. The same society runs the leper colony on Hay Ling Chau here, so he came to help the lepers here. He will operate on the policeman's hands as soon as the burns have healed enough. The doctor expects that he will be able to use his hands pretty well. He may be given a medical discharge from the police, though."

Before I left the hospital, the doctor talked to my parents and me about my burns.

"The scars will always be there. But, Joan, you can wear a soft, high collar to hide most of them. And rubbing some cocoa butter on the scars will make them more flexible."

"They will never go away?" I asked, as I looked at the doctor in his white coat over a white shirt and dark trousers. His face was solemn, and his eyes were full of kindness.

"No, they will never completely go away. And, as you grow, the scars may cause you some trouble and have to be clipped from time to time. We don't know exactly how deep the damage is, so you might have some effects internally. But I don't think so. If you do, it can be taken care of then." He motioned my parents to leave the room with him. I scarcely noticed their leaving. I was thinking about having scars on my neck. *No one will think I'm pretty with hideous scars on my neck.*

Later, I found out that the doctor had told my parents that I would not live beyond twenty-one because of the scar damage reaching my heart. But they didn't tell me that for a long time.

Chapter Seven

I went home from the hospital after a couple of weeks. I felt that my life was over. I would have scars on my neck for the rest of my days. Why even try? I wanted to die.

Christmas had come and gone before I started back to school. That day, I wore a turtleneck sweater instead of my uniform blouse. Everyone was sickly sweet to me. I enjoyed it at first, but soon I was tired of it. Then the sweater began to irritate my neck, and I felt mad with everyone in the room.

"Joan, will you go to the Sister's room, and maybe lie down until you feel better?" the teacher said.

The nurse, a young woman in a blue-and-white-striped uniform, pulled out the sweater so that it didn't rub and put a wet cloth on my neck. I lay down on the brown leather couch in her office and fell asleep. She woke me when it was time for school to be over.

"Joan, we will plan on you coming to my office anytime you feel bad. If I have stepped out, you just lie down on the couch. It will be okay," she said and smiled.

My mother was waiting with a taxi outside the school. She brought all three of us home together through the winter streets, with the kapoks' red firecracker flowers and the bahinia's orchidlike blooms showing along the way.

"How did school go?" Mum asked me as we drove along.

I told her the turtleneck wasn't the right thing to wear. It just irritated my neck. I felt better with nothing on it.

"But then, everyone would see your neck."

"Why not? Everyone knows about it anyway, and when my neck hurts, I can't stand anybody. There's no use trying to hide my neck; I don't care."

"Okay. You may wear your uniform blouse tomorrow. Is that what you want?"

"Yes."

The "phony war" was going on in Europe. Some relatives, including my uncle, were already in France ready for the German invasion. The letters we received from home all talked about the war and how it was going to soon be over, since France had strong defenses in the places where they were sure that Germany would try to invade. And London was protected from bombers by a fleet of dirigibles.

The Japanese were quiet in the area around Canton. We expected that they would leave us alone. So life continued its even pace in Hong Kong. It wasn't so bad when you got used to it.

I went for a checkup and found that my doctor had been drafted into the army and sent back to London. So I had to see someone else, and what a funny guy. He was a young man with black shiny hair, from Australia, and he had such a different accent. But also he had some news.

"Surgeons in Australia have developed some new ways to treat burns. I believe that they could improve the looks and feel of your scars. Would you consider going there for a time?" he asked Mum.

"What do you mean 'for a time'?"

"There might be a series of several small operations, so that you might have to stay for a few months."

"I'd be glad for anything to make Joan feel better about herself. But to go to Australia for months? I don't know."

My mother was quiet on the bus ride home. I knew that her mind was working to see how an expensive trip to Australia could be managed.

That night after we had gone to bed, I heard my parents talking quietly together about going to Australia. I thought about the scars on my neck. Sometimes I cried because I would never be pretty. Sometimes

I clenched my teeth and told myself, "Why try to hide them? Everybody can see them. Even if I wear a high collar, people will know that the scars are there; they come right up to my jawbone, so nothing can completely hide them." I refused to look at myself in a mirror. Sometimes I wouldn't even comb my hair, but Mother would brush my hair herself before I went out of the flat.

With spring, the "phony war" in Europe ended, with Germany invading through unexpected points, and before we could think of it, France fell. My uncle was rescued from Dunkirk's beach, but two other relatives died in France. My parents had sick hearts and sad faces most of the time, it seemed.

One evening, Father came in late from work. 'A Saam, the cook, was just carrying the food from the kitchen up the hall to the dining room, her face twisted with effort. Mum called us to come from our room, where we had been doing our homework.

We sat down, and after grace, Father began to serve the soup.

"The Japanese have invaded Hanoi in French Indochina. They seem to have been waiting until France fell to Germany and are now taking advantage of the situation in France. Perhaps they have been quiet around Canton because they were preparing for this invasion. Someone said, the Japanese really want Burma with its oil and rubber, so they are moving in that direction."

"What will happen to Hong Kong?" I asked.

"Nothing, I hope. We have no natural resources that they would want. So I think they might just bypass Hong Kong."

"However," Father continued, "this might be a good time to think about the girls in the family going to Australia. Joan could get the surgery she needs over the next several months, and by that time, we will know more about the future of Hong Kong. And I think you should fly."

Fly! I drew in my breath. We had come out by ship. It was so expensive to fly, and you could take so little luggage with you. Why did Father suggest that we go by air?

"Why fly, Father?" I asked.

"Well, I think that since you are going for just a short time, no need to spend so much time getting there. Also, you won't need to take so much stuff, since this isn't a permanent change of station. Too, you need a little excitement in your life now, don't you, Joan?"

I thought about the cousins' children who were sent to safety in Canada, but whose ship was sunk by the Germans. I wondered if Japanese submarines were active in the Pacific, as they said the German U-boats were at home.

"But what if the plane falls off the runway when it lands, like that one did here?" Emma asked.

"That was because of the storm, remember? The season for storms is past for this year, so no need to worry."

"We'll have to talk to the doctor again and see what all we need to do," Mum said.

My mother was talking as if it was already decided that we were flying to Australia.

It took several weeks to make all the arrangements. The Police Fund would help with some of the expenses. We would fly to Sydney, stopping in Singapore and Darwin on the way, then go by train to Melbourne to the hospital that specialized in burns. There was a guesthouse nearby where we would stay, and Emma and Maggie would go to school. I would have a teacher come to our rooms most of the time, but might go to regular school part of the time.

Finally, the day came when we would leave Hong Kong and Father behind. The idea of flying made my stomach curl up. Would I be sick, as we all were the first days on the boat? Tears blurred my eyes when I thought about leaving Father, but he was cheerful as he helped us to get ready.

We snapped shut our suitcases and started out the door. I wore a new blue dress and black patent shoes, although the scars showed above the high collar. I was hopeful that the scars would soon be gone.

Emma and Maggie wore their Sunday dresses and shoes. Mother put on her hat and carried her lavender spring coat over her arm. I thought her lavender-flowered dress made her look beautiful.

I called good-bye to 'A Laan and 'A Saam. They came running out of the kitchen to see us off. 'A Laan had tears in her eyes as she hugged

Maggie. They shook hands with Mother. 'A Laan would begin working for the Harrisons now, and 'A Saam would take care of Father. They knew that we would come back as soon as we could.

At the airport, a porter took the bags to the check-in counter, and Mother got out our tickets, passports, and injection records. I still felt funny in my stomach, and there was a huge lump in my throat. I saw that Emma had her arms crossed over her middle. Maggie was crying and holding Father's leg.

We waited for some time until all the passengers were checked-in, then as the loudspeaker called our flight, we got up and walked to the door. We each hugged and kissed Father, Mother last of all. Then we walked outside and climbed the stairs to the open door of the plane.

We settled into our seats, but I kept looking out the little window to see if Father was still near the door. Sometimes I caught a glimpse of him as other people came through the door and climbed up to the plane.

When all were in, the stewardess shut the door, the stairs were moved away, and the engine started. The plane began rolling to the end of the runway. I looked out at the buildings in Kowloon City on one side and the water of the bay on the other. The plane gathered speed and lifted into the air.

I kept looking down at Hong Kong as we rose. I could no longer see Father.

I didn't know then that this was the end of a part of my life. Before the surgeries were finished on my neck, all the British police wives and children were evacuated to Australia; and when I was released by the surgeon, we joined them. The scars were more flexible and less painful, but were still clearly visible above a dress collar; nothing could change that. A counselor helped me to see that I could live a good life and handle the disfigurement. I did not die at twenty-one, but am a healthy woman, married to a terrific man who says that my face is so beautiful that he never sees the scars below.

When the Japanese invaded Hong Kong in late 1941, Father was captured and interned at Stanley Prison for the duration of the war. Then, painfully thin but relatively healthy, he joined us, and we stayed in

Australia. Some of the relatives from London immigrated, and we've had a wonderful life here.

Though we are more comfortable among our own people, I remember that several Chinese people in Hong Kong helped me and took care of my sisters and my friends, gave blood for a transfusion to save Nigel's life, and rescued me from the fire. So I think kindly of them and have good memories of those years in Hong Kong. But sometimes I wonder if 'A Laan and 'A Saam suffered during the war because they had worked for the enemy. What about the Chinese sergeant? And his family? What happened to them?

The Japanese War
and Squirrel

Chapter One

December 8, 1941, in Hong Kong. A nervous policeman named AuYeung Yau Kei, affectionately nicknamed Squirrel by his close friends because of his front teeth, slurped his congee in the dining nook. The one window faced the interior courtyard, and shadows from the upper two floors made the dining nook dim most of the day. That morning it was still dark outside.

The small flat was on the ground floor, in back of the charge room and offices of the Kowloon City police station at 169 Boundary Street; it came to him and his family as part of his sergeant's pay. Of course, he was expected to answer the door and telephone during nonworking hours and do other chores for the British policemen who lived with their families in the other five flats in the building.

The sergeant was nervous because of the reported activity of the Japanese troops just over the border in South China. They had taken Canton several months previously and had been gradually working their way toward Hong Kong, about eighty miles by the road.

"Why are you up so early? It is only five o'clock, and you had the cook get up and make you congee." His wife came out of the bedroom, running her fingers through her long, black hair.

"Have you begun to pack some things?" he asked.

"Why are you on that again? The British will defend Hong Kong against the Japanese. They have all those guns up on the hills. We won't have to leave." She used his own words from long-ago conversations.

"If the Japanese don't come in by sea, what good will the guns do? They are set in concrete and can't turn. I'm beginning to think they will come in from over the border. If they do, we here on Boundary Street will be the first line of defense. You remember, the British wives and children went to Australia weeks ago."

"It's twenty miles from the border to Boundary Street. There will be plenty of time," his wife said as she disappeared into the bathroom.

The sergeant finished his breakfast and dressed. He opened the door and went out into the short hall that connected with the charge room. The one telephone in the building began ringing as he stepped into the charge room.

"Wai, wai," he said.

"The Japanese are coming over the border now. Warn …," and the telephone went dead.

He felt the tightening of his stomach in fear, but he went to each of the other five flats and gave the news to the servant who answered the door to pass on to the British officer. Then returning to the charge room, he went into his flat and talked to his wife.

"I want you and `A Fei to go to your cousin's in Macau. The Portuguese are not fighting in this war. The Japanese won't invade there. You will be safe. Wait there for me."

He looked at the sleeping child, `A Fei, and felt a hole in his heart at the idea that he wouldn't see her every day. He had a great affection for his beautiful wife, but he loved his little girl.

The sergeant heard activity in the charge room.

"I must go to work. Please take what you need, a small bag only; go to the Macau ferry now. Here is some money." He took money out of a drawer. "Send word when you get to Macau. I will come when I can. Now go."

Entering the charge room, the sergeant saw fear and anxiety on the face of each of the five British officers. Some of them had seen the blitz in England before assignment to Hong Kong, and they knew what could happen here.

"Sgt. AuYeung, go with Constable Brown. Notify every building east on Boundary Street and down into Kowloon City. When the patrolmen come, I will send them up and down Prince Edward Road. People are to stay indoors. There may be planes at any time. All schools are closed. Listen to the radio for instructions. Go, go," the Inspector directed the men.

As the two men hurried down the driveway, Sgt. AuYeung saw ahead of him his wife and daughter and watched as they flagged a taxi on Prince

Edward Road. He chuckled to himself. His wife could hurry when she wanted to.

The two policemen rang the bell and knocked at every building, then told each servant answering the summons about the invasion. Constable Brown, a young, blond man, was learning to speak Cantonese, but his tones were not good, so the sergeant did the talking. Each person was to tell everyone in his building.

The sun was burning off the light haze and, with it, the morning coolness. By noon, it would be too warm for the dark blue winter uniforms they wore. December had not yet brought winter temperatures.

A few buses and cars passed. The quiet slap, slap of the feet of the rickshaw pullers reached their ears. Dust swirled in the breeze and clogged their noses.

They worked their way down the line of small shops in the next block and turned left on Junction Road toward the walled city. Shops here weren't yet open, so they called out the warning to the open windows above the shops.

Hong Kong Police were not allowed in the walled city. Constable Brown stood a little way off, while the sergeant knocked at the open gate.

"The Japanese are crossing the border at LoWu now. We can expect planes at any time. Tell everyone to stay inside today," he told the boy standing at the gate.

As he spoke, he heard the sound of several planes coming up over Lion Rock Mountain behind him. They swooped low over the Kowloon peninsula; then came the sound of explosions on the Hong Kong side. Probably the navy yards on the Wanchai waterfront, he thought.

Together they finished the other street of shops, then returned to the station. After lunch, they would go west on Boundary Street.

It took two days for the Japanese troops from several border-crossing points to take control of the water reservoirs in the New Territories, that part leased from China in 1898 for ninety-nine years. Then on to the populated areas of Kowloon just north of Boundary Street, coming through Lion Rock Mountain by the tunnel on a commandeered train, and down Castle Peak Road by the truckload. They came to the Kowloon City police station on the third day. There had been some small-arms fire from the army camp on Waterloo Road, but the invaders soon overwhelmed them.

The British policemen cleaned out and burned records, then left ahead of the arrival of the Japanese; but Sgt. AuYeung and the patrolmen, who were Chinese, were left behind.

"Does anyone speak English?" the Japanese commander asked. He was a man in his thirties, the sergeant thought, very trim and straight, a little taller than the other Japanese soldiers.

"Yes, I do," answered the sergeant.

"Walk with me through the building," the commander said. "My name is Shimamura. Capt. Shimamura. What is your name?" he continued.

"I am Sgt. AuYeung." The sergeant explained the use of the flats and the cells in the back, and feeling that the atmosphere was not hostile, asked, "Where did you learn English? You speak it very well."

"I went to school in the United States," was the answer. "Where did you learn yours?"

"I went to an English high school here in Hong Kong."

Sgt. AuYeung and the patrolmen worked under the Japanese commander for several days. People were afraid, so stayed in their houses. There were only routine police matters, a few accidents, some scuffles at the market as supplies dwindled.

Capt. Shimamura called all the men together one morning. They gathered in the charge room and stood at attention. "My men and I will leave this station this afternoon when the army police arrive. We are being sent to the waterfront area, as the fighting is moving across the harbor to Hong Kong Island. The army police are quite strict. If you do not wish to work with the police, you may leave now."

"Why are you telling us this news?" Sgt. AuYeung paused before translating for the patrolmen.

"I would like to know if I were you," the Japanese commander said.

"Do you believe …"

"No more talk. Tell the patrolmen and get out quickly."

The sergeant translated the message, then left the charge room. He told his cook, an old woman, to leave. She was out the back door in a flash. All the other servants had left with the British officers.

It was as Squirrel that the sergeant left 169 Boundary Street by the back door. He had changed out of his uniform into the clothing of a day laborer, dirt-colored pants with the big waist lapped over the front, rolled down, and held tight by a rope, and a jacket-shirt of the same color. The jacket was open, showing a white undershirt. He carried a wicker suitcase and wore cloth shoes. All of the clothing looked worn and slightly dirty.

He walked across the street. He looked back at the 169 gate as a Japanese army car drove in. He left just in time, he thought.

He started walking along the bus line route. The street was empty and quiet. Gates were locked in the walls that surrounded every building, and shutters were closed on some of the windows he could see above the outside walls. He hadn't seen a bus since the Japanese came, but there was always a chance they might start to run. He silently thanked the cook for wrapping up some food for his lunch. He wouldn't waste money on a taxi; he could walk.

Chapter Two

Squirrel walked west along Prince Edward Road toward Nathan Road, the main street down to the point of the peninsula of Kowloon. He wanted to catch the Macau ferry, but that terminal was on the Island. With fighting moving to the Island, it would be difficult, at least for a few days.

The morning was warm and muggy, but windy. Squirrel hadn't paid attention to the weather forecasts in the newspaper or listened to the small radio in his flat. But it made him think that a storm was near. A typhoon? *Too late in the year for that,* he thought.

He saw a man struggling with the canvas awning over the door to his small store. Squirrel stopped and helped him.

"Thank you," the store owner said, then looking Squirrel in the eye, he said, "Aren't you a policeman?"

"Not anymore," Squirrel answered.

Squirrel walked on. The street was quiet; no traffic. The wind was picking up and blowing dust and grit from the street in his eyes. He thought about his wife and child. He had had no word about their arrival in Macau. He prayed that they were safe.

A foreigner stepped out of a gate in the wall just ahead of Squirrel. He jumped when he saw Squirrel. Then he began to speak in Cantonese with a Canton accent.

"Excuse me. Could you tell me if a nearby market is open? We need some food."

"The market in Kowloon City is open, but supplies are limited."

"How does one get to the market in Kowloon City?" the foreigner asked.

"Walk east on this street about two miles until you see several shops. The market is behind the shops. But there is a small store closer. It has an awning over the door."

"Thank you very much. You are kind. Do you know if the prices are higher now?"

"Yes, I know they are. And they will get higher soon."

"We are on our way back to Canton. We were stranded here because of the fighting. And with the typhoon coming, I must go out to buy food. One of our friends from Canton had to go to the hospital for an operation for appendicitis just before the invasion. He is also an American. We are worried about what will happen to us, now that Japan is at war with America."

"Japan and America are at war? I hadn't heard that."

"Japan attacked Hawaii on the same morning that they invaded Hong Kong," the American said.

"You speak Cantonese well. Have you lived in Canton long?"

"Yes, I have lived in Canton for many years. I teach in a college in Canton," the foreigner said.

Squirrel looked at the man, a little taller than Squirrel was himself. He was older, with gray in his hair and lines on his face. Squirrel had known many British people, but not many Americans. They didn't look much different, but their actions were different, he had heard; at least this man seemed to treat him as an equal.

"Thank you. You are helpful." the American man walked away toward Kowloon City.

"Sir, excuse me. There is a closer market, near the intersection of this street and Nathan Road. I don't know if it is open, but I think it may be. I will show you, if you want to walk with me."

The American stopped and looked at Squirrel. "Yes, thank you. You are kind to a stranger. The Chinese custom is for everyone to tend to his own business, not to help strangers like you are doing. Isn't that right?" The American smiled at Squirrel.

Squirrel smiled back at the American. "You're right."

45

They walked in silence for a while. Then a gust of wind blew the American's hat off. They both chased it, but Squirrel grabbed it.

"Once again, I am in your debt. Thank you. My name is Carter. May I ask your name?"

"My friends call me Squirrel. Here is the market. And it is open. I will leave you here."

Squirrel crossed the side street and walked another block to Nathan Road, then turned south toward the Island, about five miles away. Here also people walked in the narrow street, since there were no sidewalks. He made his way through the crowd, not standing out, looking no different from the others.

This area of Mong Gok was crowded with refugees from the fighting in China. *With the flats so small, it's no wonder they can't be kept inside, particularly since the actual fighting is past here,* Squirrel thought as he walked on. He felt a spray of rain hit his face; then it was raining hard, driven by the wind. He pushed into a roofed passageway with several other people.

Squirrel wished for his police raincoat, but he had left all his uniform clothes behind in the flat. He didn't even have an umbrella.

"Yau Kei, Yau Kei, is that you?"

He heard his name called. He saw a man from his church on the outer edge of the crowd holding an umbrella.

"Come, you can walk with me. Where are you going?"

Squirrel pushed his way out of the hallway to his friend, who was dressed in a business suit and leather shoes. The umbrella didn't really cover both of them, but it helped.

"Uncle Lo, I'm headed for the Macau ferry, but I know it will be a couple of days before I can go. My wife and daughter have already gone. I've left the police force. They must work under the Japanese now."

"Yes, I see. Why not come home with me tonight? Maybe the storm will be gone by tomorrow, and you can make your way to the Island then," his friend invited.

"Thanks. It isn't necessary; but thanks, that would be nice. When I left the police, I also left my flat, so I have no place," Squirrel said.

They walked on without much talk. The wind blew hard and drove the rain before it. The ground quickly turned into mud, and Squirrel's cloth shoes squished with every step.

Another few blocks, and they came to the doorway that led to a stairway to the flats over a store. They were soaked through, and glad to be out of the storm.

Inside the flat, the servant quickly brought towels and dry clothes.

"Lo Tai," Squirrel greeted his friend's wife, a short, slender, older woman in a Shanghai dress, high-collared and slit up the sides. "I'm a lot of bother to you, I'm sorry. Your husband allowed me to stop in because of the rain," he said.

Mr. Lo was as tall as Squirrel, but heavier and older. The borrowed clothes hung on Squirrel, but dry, they felt wonderful.

All the late afternoon and evening, they sat in the living room, listening to the wind and rain. The flat was one long room with brick walls, but the Los had built several three-quarter partitions to mark the various uses of the space. This was a common arrangement of lofts over stores, so Squirrel was familiar with it.

The men talked about the situation in Hong Kong, and when the leaders would give up the lost cause. The governor would do it officially, but the military leaders would make the decision.

"I heard today that the Japanese are setting up an internment center in Sham Shui Po for foreigners," Mr. Lo said.

Squirrel thought of the American he had talked to that morning. "And since the Japanese attacked Hawaii, that means that America will be in the war, and the Americans will be interned, I guess," Squirrel said.

"Most of the Americans in Hong Kong are missionaries. Do you think they will be interned also?"

"Yes, I'm afraid so. But I think it will be a surprise, since they weren't at war with Japan until last week. Our pastor wasn't expecting it, I know. He planned well, though, training members to preach and lead the congregation. Mr. Miller has been a good friend to me. He helped me through several hard times, when I was wounded and didn't have money to pay the hospital bill, and when 'A Fei was born and needed special care, and he recommended me for the police force. After all these years of speaking Cantonese, he still misses some tones, saying 'boiling' blood instead of 'precious' blood."

They laughed, then sat quietly thinking and praying about the future for their friend.

When morning came, the typhoon was still with them. The eye passed over about midmorning, then the far side of the typhoon proved to be weaker, so by late afternoon the rain had quit and the sky was clearing.

"I think I will try to go to the Island on the Jordan Road ferry. It's not far from here, it's slower, but it docks nearer to the Macau ferry than the Star Ferry does. Even though it is a vehicular ferry, passengers are allowed without vehicles. Thank you for your help during the storm. I wish you well during this occupation. Take care," Squirrel said.

He wondered if he would see his friends again. He had heard of many civilians killed in China by the Japanese, in Nanking and other cities. Would Hong Kong be as bloody?

His step quickened as he neared the ferry dock. A ferry was coming in, so the way must be clear to go to the Island. He hurried to pay his fare and get through the gate. His mind was already in Macau with his wife and child. When it was safe to go up into China from Macau, they would go to his home village. His grandparents were dead, but relatives were there who would welcome them and help them to set up a place to live.

When the blue-clad crewman opened the gate to load passengers, Squirrel paused and asked, "Is the Macau ferry still running?"

"Yes, the British are still checking traveling papers."

"How is this ferry able to get to the Island? I thought the fighting had reached there now."

"The Japanese tried to come ashore at the east end of the Island, the narrowest part of the harbor, but the storm made them go back. They will land tonight. The planes will drop bombs now that the weather is better. But we go to the west end of the Island, so are safe for a while."

The small room set aside for pedestrian passengers bulged with people. A woman with a baby on her back was trying to push her way in. Squirrel walked away to stand by the rail and look out on the harbor.

The center of the harbor, from the point of the peninsula to the Island, was just under a mile. The Jordan Road Ferry left from farther back on the west side of the peninsula, so the distance was almost twice as far. Freighters had left the buoys, so at first the harbor looked empty. But over to the left as the ferry cleared the peninsula, he could see wrecks of ships standing on end, rolled over on one side, and in other leaning positions.

Mostly Navy ships, he thought, then he saw a wrecked freighter in mid-harbor blocking passage. The bombing had practically closed the harbor.

The ferry's progress was slow. The water was choppy and the ferry wallowed from side to side. Squirrel grabbed the rail when a sudden wild lurch shook the ferry. A car rolled past him, with the driver frantically working to set the hand brake. Most of the other vehicles were trucks to help deliver supplies and rescue the injured.

As the ferry neared the Island, Squirrel saw the Macau ferry at its dock, with people crowding the deck. Would it leave before he could get there?

Chapter Three

Squirrel pushed his way to the exit gate even before the ferry docked. He was the first one off when the crewman opened the gate. He ran the nearly two blocks to the Macau ferry dock.

Two British Immigration Officers sat on the dock to check traveling papers. They worked calmly even though they was fighting a war. Many Chinese citizens in Hong Kong had no passport, so the Immigration Department had issued them traveling papers.

Squirrel took out his papers from the day he had entered Hong Kong. As a policeman, he had a resident's card, but he didn't want to use that card to leave the Colony . He had a long line of people in front of him.

"This will be the last ferry to Macau before the Japanese take over," he heard a man in front of him say. Surely, he would be able to get on, he thought. He must. A big lump was blocking his breathing.

The line crawled forward. He was thankful that he had insisted that his wife and daughter leave earlier. Children in the line were tired, cross, and tearful. Little ones were carried on the mother's, or an amah's, back. These soon went to sleep, rocked by the woman's motion.

Eventually, Squirrel got to the table for his papers to be checked.

The two British officers looked briefly at the papers, then stamped them. Why were they even checking papers? To Squirrel, it seemed to be a useless process. Of course, the Portuguese would check them again in Macau.

He walked up the gangway and pushed his way through the crowded deck. He found an unoccupied spot near the prow of the boat. He could look over the rail and down to the water.

He had been on the ferry only a few minutes when the gates were closed and the gangway pulled up; preparations were made for casting off.

The engines started, and the ferry moved away from the dock. This ferry was a riverboat formerly used in China that had left Canton ahead of the Japanese takeover. Now, it was leaving Hong Kong just before the Japanese took control. It was built with several small cabins on each side and a wide, open deck on the front and aft of the boat.

The water in the harbor was still choppy from the typhoon, but the ferry soon was out in open waters that were calmer. They skirted Laantau, a long island with high peaks and largely uninhabited. Squirrel saw Lamma Island, and Cheung Chau Island off to the left. He had been to Cheung Chau once with his family. It was a vacation spot for many foreign families living in China. He remembered how 'A Fei had played in the sand with a little black-haired white girl who spoke Cantonese well. His heart ached to see 'A Fei and her mother. Then he told himself, *I'll be with them soon.*

The ferry was barely out of Hong Kong waters when the planes came. The passengers on the deck heard them first, then saw about ten planes coming down the Pearl River toward them. The planes turned left and went down the harbor, dropping bombs as they went. *There must be nothing left of the headquarters in Wanchai,* Squirrel thought. The planes went out of sight around the east end of the Island, then came back, machine-gunning the streets. Two planes flew low over the ferry, but no bullets landed on them. Then the planes banked to the right and disappeared up the river to Canton.

The passengers breathed sighs of relief.

They had just rounded a small island in international waters when a Japanese patrol boat came from behind the island. The patrol boat fired a shell across the front, and the ferry stopped. An officer and two men boarded, talked to the Captain, looked at papers, and then left the ferry. As soon as the men were off, the motor started, and the ferry went on its way to Macau.

The sun dropped below the mountains on the China coast, and it was soon dark. Some people were buying rice boxes from the vendor on board. Squirrel pulled out the food his cook had made for him the day before and the things that Mrs. Lo had added when he left their flat. Sitting on his heels, he ate for a while, then was conscious of eyes watching him. He looked up and saw a little girl watching him steadily. Suddenly he knew she was hungry and had no food. He held out the container of cold rice.

She reached in for a handful, shaped it carefully into a ball, and popped it into her mouth. As she ate it, a lovely smile appeared on her face. They shared the rest of the rice.

The whole forty-mile trip would take six to seven hours. If stopped again by another Japanese patrol, it might take longer.

Squirrel sat down on the deck. Soon, he was nodding. Other passengers sat on the deck, and some were sleeping. These past days had been stressful for everyone. Now, they had left the war and hoped to find refuge in peaceful Macau.

Squirrel was back at 169 Boundary Street in their little flat. 'A Fei climbed into his lap, telling him about her day at school. 'A Fei had lost her first baby tooth, and she was concerned that it might not grow in as the teacher said it would. Squirrel laughed at 'A Fei's worry and reassured her. The cook called them to eat, and the Beautiful Wife, 'A Fei, and he sat down to eat together. He felt so happy. Then suddenly, a loud explosion blew the flat apart, and his wife and daughter were gone. He frantically hunted for them, but they were nowhere to be found.

Someone shook Squirrel's shoulder. He opened his eyes and looked around. It was only a dream.

He was shaken by the dream. His arms and legs felt like lead. He dragged himself up and leaned against the rail.

The night was dark, and he couldn't see where they were on the trip. No lights showed on any of the small islands that littered the estuary of the river. It's no wonder that pirates had used these islands as hideouts for hundreds of years. Even in 1580, when Macau was given to the Portuguese, it was payment for a one-time ridding the area of pirates.

Squirrel sat again on his heels and thought about the vivid dream. It had been so real. He prayed that it would never come true.

He slept again and was still asleep when the ferry reached Macau. People began to move, gathering their belongings. The Portuguese Immigration men came on board, set up their table, and began checking passports and traveling papers.

The crew had gathered up the passports, and these were piled on the table, with any Portuguese passports checked first. Last of all were the traveling papers for the Chinese passengers.

Squirrel waited patiently for his turn. He was in Macau at last and would see his family soon. After his papers were checked, he walked off the ferry, down the gangway, and out onto the street. Even that late at night, pedicab drivers were still hoping for a fare. These bicycles, with a two-wheeled seat behind, were different from the traditional rickshaw pulled by a man, and showed the long European influence.

Motioning, Squirrel climbed in the seat of the first one, put his wicker suitcase beside him, and told the driver the address of his wife's cousin. Lights along the street and in stores here were bright. They didn't fear a Japanese attack, he thought, since Portugal was neutral. They rode along the Praya Grande, the broad street on the waterfront, in the soft darkness.

Squirrel thought of the times he had come to Macau with his father from their village not far across the border in China. Most of the vegetables that people in his village grew were sold to Macau markets. The village also had a small factory that made dishes, and these were sold to an agent in Macau. Squirrel's father spoke some Portuguese and acted as a go-between in the sales. It was his father that sent Squirrel to a mission school, then to board at the Diocesan Boys' School, an English high school in Hong Kong. Squirrel became a Christian, and after a long time his parents allowed his baptism, although they didn't change their own beliefs. They felt that their son had just added another belief to the traditional Buddhism and Taoism, as well as the family ancestor worship.

Macau had a different feel to it than Hong Kong, he thought. The streets were wider, the pace was slower, and the pastel-painted houses had a different look. A blank wall with a gate greeted the visitor, but inside the wall was a courtyard filled with flowers and active people.

The pedicab driver turned off the Praya on a narrow side street and up a slight hill to a small park, past a cemetery and a small church. Squirrel knew this was the cemetery where Robert Morrison, the first Protestant missionary to China, was buried. Morrison had translated the Bible into Chinese under hard circumstances, and later served as a translator for the British in settling their war with China. That was when Hong Kong was ceded to the British.

They came to the base of a high hill. He could see the façade of St. Paul's Cathedral, built by Christian refugees from Japan when their government had thrown them out of Nagasaki in the early 1600s. Two centuries later, in 1835, the cathedral burned, and since then only the façade remained. But high on one hill, it shared the skyline with the fort on the other hill. Once a Hong Kong governor looking at the façade wrote a hymn, *In the Cross of Christ I Glory.*

His wife's cousin lived beyond the cathedral just below the fort. The pedicab driver stopped a little way up the hill. "Too steep to take you farther," he said, puffing.

Squirrel picked up his suitcase and stepped out of the pedicab. He would walk the block remaining—then he was running, hurrying to know his wife and little girl were safe.

Chapter Four

The gate was locked and the house was dark when Squirrel got there. He punched the bell and heard it ring in the distance. All was quiet. He hit the bell again, and heard it ring again. Then a light came on, and soon the old gateman jogged down the walk.

"Who is it? Who is it?" he grumbled.

"AuYeung Yau Kei," Squirrel answered. "Did my wife and daughter get here last week? I've heard nothing."

"Yes, yes, they are here. And now, you've come from Hong Kong. How is it there?"

Squirrel heaved a sigh of relief. He didn't realize how much he'd worried about them until he knew they were safe.

"Not good. Not good. The Japanese are about to take it. They control Kowloon, and will take the Island soon. I left on the last ferry to Macau."

"Come in. Come in." The old man unlocked the gate and opened it. He took the wicker suitcase from Squirrel, then shut and locked the gate again. Together they walked up to the house, talking about the situation in Hong Kong.

The house was a long, low, stone building on the side of the steep hill up to the fort. The gate was near the lower edge of the garden, and the walk sloped up to the house through the plants and flowers. On the far side of the garden, near the kitchen, was a vegetable garden.

Once in the house, a servant led him down a hall, past a large main room filled with black wooden chairs and small, carved tables, to the bedroom where his wife and child slept. They had a joyous reunion, the three of them, with 'A Fei jumping up and down on the bed. Squirrel and his wife didn't sleep much the rest of the night, talking and loving. When 'A Fei jumped in bed with them the next morning, they were slow getting up.

"What do you hear about the situation in our village?" Squirrel asked the cousin, older than he was, with a white scraggly beard, as they ate breakfast. "I thought that might be the safest place for us to go."

"The Japanese do not control this side of the river; China does. They do control the border with Macau. In some places, even on the Hong Kong side of the river, the control is thin. They don't have enough men to have tight control everywhere. Your village is still in Chinese hands. That might be a good place to go. You are welcome here, even though we are your wife's relatives so I know that you would hate to ask, but other relatives will probably come soon and will need a place. But do what you think is best."

They stayed three days more in Macau, buying supplies, packing, and getting the right papers to go into China. Then they said good-bye to the cousin and his family, loaded everything into two pedicabs, and went the short distance to the border.

Two Portuguese guards glanced at their bags, raised the arm, and motioned them through. On the other side, two Japanese guards carefully inspected the baggage, opening every bit, searching thoroughly before allowing them to take the bags from the pedicabs and carry them to the China side. Squirrel hired two rickshaw men to take them and the bags to the bus stop, about two miles away.

When the bus rattled up in a cloud of dust, they pushed their way on, throwing their bags up on top of the bus with other bags. Squirrel climbed up to the top himself, to be sure their bags were tied down and wouldn't bounce off on the bumpy road.

The winter countryside didn't look much different from a summer scene. Only a few trees had dropped their leaves, and no leaves had changed colors. The jacaranda's spikes of purple flowers and the bahinia's orchidlike blossoms welcomed the cooler weather. The rice harvest was over, and paddies were being prepared for spring planting. Under the clear blue skies, water buffaloes pulled plows across paddies, and men stooped in the fields. On one hillside, dark green ceramic jars, each about two feet tall and containing the bones of ancestors, sat in irregular rows.

They rode for about an hour until they came to the home village of the AuYeung family. A few miles farther on was Chong Shan, the birthplace of Sun Yat Sen, who had also studied in Hong Kong as a youth.

Squirrel, the Beautiful Wife and 'A Fei got down from the bus, retrieved their bags from the roof of the bus, and started for the Big House. A man pushing a two-wheeled cart walked toward them.

"Help with the bags?" the man asked.

"Yes, we do need help," Squirrel said and began placing the bags on the flat top of the cart. "We are going to the Big House."

They walked along together, down the one street of the village. They passed a medicine shop and a restaurant with the front open to the street and tables both inside and out. Open stalls sold cabbages, bak tsoi, tomatoes, and other vegetables, and pyramids of oranges. One had a display of fresh meat and live chickens. Smells from the chickens crowded out the tangy smell of the oranges. The last two stalls sold cloth and books. The cold wind raised little whirlwinds of dust that filled their mouths and noses with grit.

High walls enclosed the homes on both sides of the dirt street, with trees showing above and even some branches hanging over into the street. Beyond the last house on the street, they could see the Big House. It was two stories, built of bricks in a U-shape. He remembered with sadness that his father intended to finish the fourth side of the square that his grandfather had built, but the fighting between Cheng Kai Shek and the local warlords had delayed the building, as well as taking the life of his father, who had joined in the battle. Squirrel and his mother had remained in Canton until her death several years later.

An uncle and his family lived in the Big House now. But Squirrel knew that he and his family would be welcome and room would be found for them. He relished the peace of the village and the security of knowing he was at home.

He rang the bell at the gate, and a servant came to answer the summons.

"'A Saam, how are you?" Squirrel greeted the wife of the old gateman he remembered from his grandparents' time. She stumped along on the crippled feet that long ago had been bound, and now, even unbound, were tiny and stiff.

"A long time since we've seen you," `A Saam answered as she opened the gate. The gateman hurried up behind her and began to lift the bags down from the cart.

They walked across the garden to the door in the middle of the back wall. The building's arms extended out on each side of the garden. `A Saam opened the door and called to a servant inside to come help with the bags. Squirrel's uncle came out of the room on the right of the hall to see what the noise was about.

"Nephew, how good it is to see you and your family. What is the situation in Hong Kong?" He was a middle-aged man, his hair thinning on top, and his stomach bulged out of his black lacquered cotton jacket and pants.

"Very bad; I'm afraid the Japanese will take the city in a few days. I sent my wife and daughter to her cousin's in Macau last week, but now I have left the police since the police must work for the Japanese. We felt it was safer to be here in our village."

"The Japanese do not control this area, and may never," the uncle answered. "This is not an industrial area, and as long as we grow food and live peacefully, they may let us alone. Come in, come in."

They walked into the large main room, with the same black wood chairs and tables that the cousin in Macau had, and sat down. The servants put the bags down in the hall.

"Upstairs, on the left arm, there are two rooms with a small kitchen and servant's room. Would that be satisfactory for you and your family? They haven't been used since your parents went to Canton and will need to be cleaned."

"Yes, that will be fine. You are kind, Uncle."

The next few days, they settled in the upstairs rooms. The large room they used as a sitting room. It had open slits about six inches long high up in the outside corner. The slits had once been used as gun ports for defense of the house and occupants. There was an upstairs alcove that `A Fei could use as a bedroom. The kitchen had a tiled bench to hold a small charcoal burner and a sink with a drain. Water would have to be carried up from the well in the garden. The next room had a tiled square, with a drain to use as a bath, when a person soaped down, then rinsed by pouring water on themselves. All the walls were plastered inside and painted a light tan color. The last room was a bedroom for Squirrel and the Beautiful Wife. It would become a comfortable place for them.

Squirrel got a job as a night watchman at the market. One night he picked up a scrap of paper. It turned out to be part of a newspaper and told that Hong Kong had surrendered to the Japanese on December 25, 1941.

They had been in the village several weeks when two men came to visit Squirrel. They appeared to be Chinese peasants, but looking closely, he saw that one was a former policeman and the other was a British officer in disguise.

"Sgt. AuYeung," the British man began, "I understand that you are a good, honest man, and willing to help people in need."

Squirrel smiled to himself. He knew that beginning with a compliment was the best way to set up a request for help.

"Yes, thanks to God's grace, I try to be that sort of person."

"Perhaps you are aware that in Hong Kong, all foreigners have been confined to the prison at Stanley or in a former army camp in Shum Shui Po on the Kowloon side. Some other officers, as well as myself, have escaped from Shum Shui Po camp. We hooked up with Chinese guerrillas in the New Territories, and the others have made their way into Free China. I stayed behind to help more escape, if possible. Now, you speak English, as well as Mandarin and Cantonese. You know the New Territories, too. Would you consider helping?"

Squirrel didn't answer. He and his family were safe. They had a comfortable place to live and some money. Why should he risk his life, and perhaps his family? This war might last a long time. The Japanese had been fighting in China since 1937. So far, they were winning. Some people said, now that America was in the war, things would be different. But would they? His uncle's small battery-powered radio regularly reported that people were still being killed, soldiers were fighting, and planes were dropping bombs in West China. He didn't see how his help could make a difference.

Chapter Five

"You remember Pastor Miller? Didn't you go to his church?" The Chinese policeman spoke for the first time. "The last men who escaped told us that there was no medicine in Shum Shui Po camp, and that Pastor Miller was very sick and may die if medicine is not brought in. Could you do that much?"

Pastor Miller! Squirrel thought of the help Pastor Miller had given him, with money when `A Fei was sick, the recommendation for the police force, and other things. Now he was sick and needed medicine.

"Of course, I can do that. What is the medicine, and how do I get it to him?"

"We bought the medicine in Chong Shan as we came through this morning. Here it is. When can you take it to him?" The British officer was in charge. He handed a small package to Squirrel. They had known that Squirrel would want to help Pastor Miller, he thought.

"The best way would be a fishing boat from Chong Shan. They can get close into the shore near Shum Shui Po. You would have to swim a short distance. I know that you were a champion swimmer in middle school. That shouldn't bother you." The foreigner gave more instructions.

After the men were gone, Squirrel sat thinking about the trip back to Hong Kong. His wife came in the room, and looking at him, she asked, "Who were they, and what did they want?"

He told her about what they wanted him to do.

"Husband, you must not do this. Just today in the market, I found some bread that had been brought in. I bought one loaf, just for a change, and gave it to `A Fei to hold carefully. I turned back to the clerk, and then

I heard 'A Fei cry out. A man had taken the loaf out of her arms and run away. I told her not to cry, that the man was hungry and needed the bread more than we did. If people here are stealing food, it will be much worse in Hong Kong. There is danger not only from the Japanese, but from the Chinese who are hungry."

"Yes, I've heard people in the market talking. I know that food is already scarce in Hong Kong. But think of Pastor Miller needing the medicine that I have in my hand. If he doesn't get it, he will die. How can I not go to help a man who has been such a friend to me?"

He looked over the few things he brought from Hong Kong. Yes, there was the small, waterproof silk envelope. He could put the medicine in it. He would need something to put his clothes in while he swam the last bit. He must have dry clothes to put on after the swim. A wet-through person in winter would be easy to spot, as well as suffer from the cold.

He picked up the sack with the medicine in it. Besides the bottle with pills, there was a thin, waterproof sack with arm straps that could be worn like a knapsack, and a small electric torch. They were confident of his agreement even before they talked to him.

He spent a restless afternoon, thinking, praying, and walking around. He should sleep a while, but couldn't. He went to see the other watchman at the market and arranged to be off. He played with 'A Fei, keeping the shuttlecock in the air with the sole of his foot. 'A Fei had trouble with the cock, but kept trying. The Beautiful Wife wasn't talking to him since he told her he had to go.

About dark that evening, he walked into Chong Shan, then to the waterfront to find the fishing boats. One was watching for him and waved to catch his attention. He climbed aboard the boat, which smelled of their product, and they cast off.

The Pearl River narrowed upstream, so the crossing here would be only about four hours. Squirrel found a pile of canvas and lay down to rest. He dropped off to sleep and was still sleeping soundly when the captain shook his shoulder.

"We are coming in as close as we can to Shum Shui Po. You can see the lights from here."

Squirrel quickly got out of his clothes, folded them into the sack, put it on his back, and was ready. He arranged to meet the boat the next night, in the same location. He would watch for their signal and would answer with the electric torch from the shore.

The water was cold, but he swam out, his strokes clean and economical. Before long, he was tiring. He hadn't swum such a distance since his school days. He floated on his back to rest. Then he swam again. As he tired the second time, he felt something against his feet. Whatever it was lifted him on its back and carried him along. Ah, the white dolphins! He had never swum with one, but of course, they followed fishing boats, and this one thought he was playing with it. It dumped him off in shallow water.

He lay in the water and looked at the shoreline. No movement of any kind. He saw some boats turned upside down on the sandy beach near where the short trees came right down to the water. He moved silently through the water, then ran bent over to the boats. He hurried into the trees, stopped to dry off, and dressed, then buried the waterproof sack and wet things in the sand under a boat.

He walked quietly through the trees up to the street, then stopped to look around and get his bearings. He saw that he wasn't far from the army cantonment that now served as an internment camp for foreigners. He watched for a time. All was quiet. He would wait for first light before moving up to the fence. The men had told him that several Chinese would approach the fence then and sell foodstuffs or other things to the prisoners. He would pass the medicine to one of the prisoners to give to Pastor Miller. Perhaps Mrs. Miller would come out to the fence if they expected the medicine today. He hoped that Mrs. Miller would be there. It would be good to see her, and he could be sure that Pastor Miller got what he needed.

It was perhaps an hour before he heard someone else coming quietly to the fence. Then others began to appear. On the other side of the fence, prisoners silently walked to the barrier. Squirrel watched until he saw a woman approach the fence. He wasn't sure it was Mrs. Miller, but moved up to the fence. Yes, it was his pastor's wife. He felt a tightness in his chest to see her in worn, mismatched clothes that hung on her thin frame.

"Sz Mo," he said just above a whisper, "how are you? Here is the medicine that Pastor Miller needs." He passed it through a hole in the wire.

"Yau Kei, it's good to see you. Are you and your family well?"

"Yes, we are living in my home village, and all is good with us. I hope you will not be here long."

"I hear that we are to be exchanged soon. Thank you for the medicine. Don't put yourself in danger any longer. Thank you. God bless you and your family. Good-bye."

She walked away from the fence with the bottle of medicine and did not look back. Other prisoners did the same as they quietly returned to their quarters. Squirrel moved away from the fence, melting into the group of sellers.

He now had a whole day to wait for the return on the fishing boat. Where would he be safe? If he went to the home of a friend, then was caught, he would bring trouble to the friend. Slowly he walked back to the beach, then to the overturned boats. They were still in the same position, and as he looked he realized that the boats hadn't been moved for some days, maybe weeks. He scooted under a boat, felt warm and safe in spite of the cool, damp sand, and the moldy smell of the boat, and went to sleep.

It was late afternoon when Squirrel awoke. He heard shouting and shooting from somewhere, so he lay still. The noise was far enough away that he couldn't make out what was being said. Then it was quiet again.

His stomach growled, telling him it was time to eat. He searched his memory for a place to eat in this area. Maybe there would be a street stall selling noodles in soup.

Carefully, he inched out from under the boat, and into the scrubby trees. He walked up to the street, then north to a cross street where stalls were set up for business. Many stalls were empty, a few sold vegetables, and other foodstuff. On the far side of the area he saw a table set up with a charcoal burner nearby cooking noodles. Yes, this was what he needed.

He ate one bowl of watery soup with only a few noodles, and wanted another. But he decided that the long swim coming up would go better with a leaner stomach. He looked around the market area and saw two Japanese soldiers coming. He felt a tight band of fear in his chest, but he got up and slowly moved away from the table, looked at some items for sale, and then still not hurrying, walked to the street and back toward the shore and the boats. There he slept again, dreaming that he could see the boat, but couldn't reach it. He kept trying to swim closer, but the boat moved away each time.

When it was dark he went into the trees and looking at the moon and stars figured the time. He still had some time to wait. He dug up the waterproof sack with the electric torch and swim trunks from the sand, then sat down leaning against a tree. The sound of the waves soothed him, and after a time, he nodded. Then he jerked awake, checked the stars, and looked out into the channel. He had better move around some, or he'd sleep through his date with the fishing boat.

Chapter Six

Several boats appeared in the bay off Shum Shui Po, their lights glittering in the darkness. Squirrel took off his clothes, put on the trunks, packed his clothes in the waterproof sack, tied it on his back, and watched for the signal. The cold wind found him in the trees and circled around him. He shivered as he watched. There was the signal, three short flashes of the light. He grabbed the electric torch and sent the signal back.

He walked out in the shallow water, then stretched out swimming. He felt stronger than the night before, but he had to rest once; then the dolphins found him again but just swam alongside of him until he was near the boat. He felt a surge of affection for the beautiful creatures, white in the water, but pink when they jumped out of the water to cool their bodies.

At the boat, the crew let down a rope ladder. Once on the boat, he dressed again, then found his previous bed on the tarps, and slept until they tied up in Chong Shan.

The sun was rising from the China Sea when Squirrel got home. He crept into the bedroom and found the Beautiful Wife asleep, but she smiled when he got into bed and put his arm around her.

"Never again," she said as she kissed him.

About a week later, the former policeman came again. Two British officers wanted to escape Shum Shui Po camp and needed a guide to the New Territories, where they would meet the guerrillas.

"Why now?" Squirrel asked.

"Several prisoners are to be exchanged for Japanese prisoners from the United States soon. When they leave, all the rest of the prisoners will be transferred to Stanley Prison, where there will be no escape possible. Also, the longer the prisoners are interned, the weaker they become, so getting away is harder."

Squirrel thought of the way Mrs. Miller had lost weight in just a few weeks. Probably all were like that.

"There is this, too. One of the men was wounded in the fighting and left on a street near the waterfront. A Japanese patrol found him after a day or two, and instead of shooting him, they did first aid, then brought him to the camp. Otherwise, he would have died."

Might have been Captain Shimamura, Squirrel thought; *he was sent to the waterfront when he was transferred from Boundary Street.*

"How can he escape from the camp? Can he walk?" Squirrel asked.

"Oh, yes, he can walk, but he is not strong. Perhaps you could get them to the fishing boat, then out to the New Territories."

Squirrel thought about how the dolphins had helped him. Perhaps it could happen again. But there were the boats left on the beach. It would be better to take a boat rather than expect the man to swim.

He was thinking about it as if he had already agreed to the project. He knew that the Beautiful Wife would not like it at all. He realized that this was not the end of the projects that they would ask him to help with. This was just the beginning.

They worked out arrangements and the men left.

That night, Squirrel again walked into Chong Shan. It was a still, cold night, and his coat felt good. Down on the waterfront, he found the same fishing boat, made his way to the pile of canvas, and slept until the boat was near Shum Shui Po. He felt the tide going in as he swam and reached the little beach without tiring. The dolphins were not around the fishing boat this time, but he hadn't needed them.

The boats were still in the same location near the trees. He hurried into the trees and dressed. Then he inspected the boats as well as he could in the dark, choosing the one that he thought best to use.

The men were to come to the trees at three o'clock. He didn't know how or when they were planning to leave the camp. The fishing boat would wait, appearing to fish, until nearly four o'clock, when the tide would be going out. Looking at the moon and stars, he saw that he had nearly an hour to wait. He found a comfortable tree to lean against and went to sleep.

A tree limb snapping woke Squirrel. He didn't move until he saw two men among the trees, one helping the other.

Rising up from where he sat, he spoke just above a whisper. "Where are you going?"

"Going fishing," was the answer.

Squirrel motioned for the men to follow him. They stepped out into the cold wind on the beach just above the boats. Squirrel signaled the fishing boat with the electric torch, then went to the sampan he had selected and motioned for the two men to help turn the boat up. Then they pushed it down into the water, and after helping the injured man in, the second man got on. Then Squirrel pushed it until it was well out into the waves. He jumped on, then stood and poled toward the fishing boat.

Pong! A bullet smacked into the side of the sampan. Squirrel dropped flat into the boat. "Get down," he said.

Another bullet hit the boat. Had the Japanese patrol seen them? Who else could be shooting?

"Hey, it's leaking," the second man spoke.

"See if you can find something to bail with," Squirrel answered.

The man crawled around on the bottom of the sampan but found nothing.

"It's coming in pretty fast," he said.

"We're going to have to swim for it," Squirrel said.

The men took off their shoes and coats. Squirrel wished he had not left his trunks and waterproof sack on the beach.

"You just float on your back, and I will tow you," Squirrel said to the injured man. "We don't have far to go." He put his left hand under the man's chin and swam with his right arm in the cold water.

The men headed for the lights of the fishing boat. The lights seemed farther away than they had just a moment ago.

And there were the dolphins wanting to play. One came up between Squirrel and his tow, taking both of them on his back. The second man was startled by a dolphin nudging him and squealed, but was then happy to ride, too.

Once near the fishing boat, the dolphins dumped the men and went on with their play. The crew helped the men aboard.

The boat captain was prepared with a stack of old, worn, peasant clothes. They dressed, then the two foreigners blackened their faces, and all laid down to rest.

The boat headed west toward Canton, but stopped in midstream just after they passed the Chinese border. A sampan came out from shore, and the two escapees were helped down into it. Squirrel told them good-bye and stayed with the fishing boat back to Chong Shan.

Walking home on the path through the trees, he thought about his activities. Was he going to continue helping escapees? His blood sang with the adrenaline rush that he was useful to God and to his fellow man. But the Beautiful Wife did not like it one bit. Was it fair to her and 'A Fei to risk his life? Was it any more of a risk than police work was?

A lamp shone in the window when he got home. Something must be the matter with 'A Fei. He ran up the stairs and along the passage, then burst into the bedroom. 'A Fei was in their bed, and the Beautiful Wife bending over her.

"What is it?" he asked.

"'A Fei has a fever, and her neck hurts her. I'm scared that it is the paralyzing disease of children. What if it is?"

Oh, God, spare 'A Fei. She's our only child.

"I heard in Chong Shan yesterday that a foreign missionary nurse was still in a village on the other side of the city. Since the Chinese still control this area, she hasn't been sent to a camp. Maybe she would know what to do. I'll go hunt for her now."

He hurried out of the house and back along the way he had just come. It was daylight, but overcast, and a strong wind out of the north had started. He always felt that wind came directly from Siberia, and the Great Wall just north of Peking did nothing to stop it.

He pulled the collar of his jacket up over his ears and walked quickly up the narrow path, through the East Gate, past the closed market area, and on down the street to the West Gate of Chong Shan. He'd never been on the west side of the city, so he looked at the buildings he passed. More businesses than the village, but not as many as Hong Kong or even

Macau. He asked directions several times from other early risers before he found his way to the village where a foreign nurse lived and worked in a small clinic.

It was almost noon when he found Miss Red. That wasn't her English name, but was so much easier to say that even in English, people called her that. She was tall, taller than he was himself, with brown hair and a well-padded frame.

"My daughter has a fever, and her neck is hurting and stiff. Does she have that paralyzing disease?" Squirrel asked.

"Let me get some things, and I'll come with you. I was in America last year; just returned in October. While I was there, I learned a new method of treating the paralyzing disease after the fever is gone. Putting hot cloths on the affected parts seems to lessen the paralysis. We'll do what we can."

They hired two rickshaws and urged the men to run through Chong Shan back to the village.

`A Fei's fever was still high when they got to the Big House. Miss Red washed her with cool, wet cloths and gave her half of the last aspirin she had.

"Are there any other children who are sick?" Miss Red asked.

"I'll ask around the neighbors," Squirrel said as he left the room.

He couldn't hide the alarm he felt as he questioned everyone he met.

"No one in the village is sick, but someone said that he had heard several children were sick in Macau. We were in Macau some time ago. Did she catch it then?" he told Miss Red when he returned.

"Doctors still don't know how it's transmitted. We just have to work with the results of the disease and hope to lessen the damage," Miss Red said.

Chapter Seven

They hardly slept, sponging 'A Fei, asking her to drink some water. Squirrel hunted all over Chong Shan for a bottle of Coca-Cola when 'A Fei wished for one.

The uncle and his family stayed in their part of the house. All wastes were to be taken far away. One morning, the uncle yelled up from the garden when he saw Squirrel outside his door, "Might as well let her die. She'll be a cripple, and no man will marry her. All you can do is sell a cripple to the beggars."

"Never!" Squirrel answered.

Then one morning, 'A Fei was clear-eyed and cool. The fever was over, and the work of keeping her from being paralyzed began.

They took turns keeping the hot towels on her legs, which seemed to be the place of the heaviest damage. Miss Red finally slept after she satisfied herself that they knew how to keep water hot, and how to wring out the towels and still keep them hot. 'A Fei sometimes cried because the cloths were so hot, but Miss Red and her parents kept on.

Then came the day that Miss Red got 'A Fei out of bed and helped her to stand. She took a couple of steps, and her legs held her. Hallelujah! Praise God! Squirrel and the Beautiful Wife shouted their relief. The uncle and all the rest of the family now crowded in to share in the joy.

Miss Red stayed a day or two longer, then returned to her village and the clinic.

'A Fei was weak, and had to rest often, but she was alive and she was walking. Squirrel was so full of joy that his face always had a smile.

The former Hong Kong policeman came again. Squirrel was glad for the opportunity to help someone else since God had been so good to him.

"Several British navy men tried to escape the Japanese on an old navy ship just before the surrender, but they were captured and brought back to Hong Kong. An admiral is among the ones brought to Shum Shui Po camp. He had been on his way to meet with Cheng Kai Shek to talk about the defense of West China, Burma, and India, but was caught here by the fighting. It's vital that he escape before he can be made to talk, since he knows so much about the British defense plans for Burma and India," the former policeman said to Squirrel.

"Will we do as we did before?"

"They saw you the last time. Maybe someone told them about the fishing boat, because the Japanese will not let them fish near to the shore now. You will have to find another way into Hong Kong Once you are there, we have arranged for you to drive a garbage truck to the camp and then out into the New Territories. You will be a garbage man.. Ha!"

Late that afternoon, Squirrel walked through Chong Shan and down to the pier and talked to the captain of the fishing boat about how he could reach the other shore since the fishing boat could not get close to Shum Shui Po.. They agreed that he could get a rubber raft, or something like that, bring it on the boat, and then when he was ready, they would help him launch the raft. He went back to the shops on the waterfront and asked for a rubber raft, but there was no such thing in Chong Shan. Finally, an old man sitting on a pile of rope and smoking a pipe spoke up. His grandson had a small raft made of five or six poles that he used to push out from the bank when he went fishing. Would that work?

"Could I see it?" Squirrel asked.

They walked past several streets and came to a small house with a wall around it at the end of one street. Inside the wall was a small, bare courtyard. Leaning on one wall were a few bamboo poles about six feet long, tied into a raft, each pole about an inch apart from the others but tied tighter together at each end so that they curled up a little. Squirrel picked it up and found that he could carry it on his shoulder.

"Does it float?" he asked.

"You can try it out, if you want."

They went down to the river's edge, Squirrel carrying the raft. He put it in the water, and it did float.

"Is there a paddle or a pole?"

"Yes, there are both."

The sale was agreed to. Squirrel paid the price and walked away to the fishing boat with the raft on his shoulder. He felt better with the problem of getting to Hong Kong solved.

The fishing boat made an upper crossing where the river narrows that night, and the crew helped Squirrel launch the little raft. He stood and propelled the craft with the long pole that ended in a wide blade like an oar. The boat left, heading for better fishing grounds down the estuary. It was very quiet then, and he could hear only the soft movement of the pole in the water. He could see the shore in the pale moonlight. This was near the spot where the last two escapees had met the sampan. He wondered if anyone would be there to meet him. Probably not, since he was Chinese in his own territory and able-bodied. They would expect him to handle it all himself.

The raft ran up on the narrow beach. He jumped out and pulled it up to where he could hide it in the reeds and rocks, then started walking inland, hunting for a road or even a path. He planned to walk over the border to the Hong Kong side, then catch the first bus into Kowloon at about five o'clock.

He found a sandy track in the tall grass and scrub bushes. In the dim light of the moon, he saw that it paralleled the coastline. He'd walked about an hour on it when he came to the small stream that marked the border between China and Hong Kong. If he couldn't find a boat to borrow, he'd wade across; it was that shallow. He walked along the bank for a short distance, then found a wooden box, a little longer than it was wide, about three feet by four feet, with a two-inch railing around it. Someone must use it to ferry vegetables across to sell in Hong Kong, because there were clods of dirt still on the top.

He pushed it into the stream, got on it himself, and used his hand to push out from the bank. The shove sent him almost across the stream, and in a moment he had jumped off and pulled the box up on that bank. He'd use it again on his way back home.

He found a path through the six-inch-tall grass that was leaning over from the sea wind. The path was well-worn; it had been used, he guessed, by others on their way into Hong Kong. Every time disasters—wars, drought, or floods—erupted in China, refugees poured into Hong Kong, and there was no guard point here. He smiled to himself. As a young policeman, just out of the academy, he was stationed in Yeun Long, the nearest town. He sniffed the air. Yes, by the mixed onion-human waste smell, he could tell Yeun Long was nearby. No place else in Hong Kong smelled like Yuen Long, since onions were a major crop around here.

It was in Yuen Long that he met the Beautiful Wife. He found a small Christian fellowship meeting in a house. Usually, he was off on Sunday and went into Kowloon for church, but one Sunday he was on duty. He walked by the house and stood outside listening to the music.

"Why are you checking on the Christians? It's not against the law to meet for worship." The angry voice came from the most beautiful mouth, he saw, as he turned around to face his accuser.

"No, no. I'm just listening to the music for a few minutes," he said. " And besides, I'm a believer myself." That brought a smile to the beautiful face, and she invited him into the service, too.

He laughed to himself as he thought about that time and the things that had happened after that first meeting, ending up with their marriage and life together.

He walked on until he came across the paved road where the bus ran. He followed the road for two or three miles until he came to a bus stop. There were only scattered houses along the road at this point, not one in sight from the bus stop. He sat down on his heels to wait. A faint light was breaking in the east, so the first bus would come before long.

Several others joined him at the bus stop before the bus came, and it was already full. Squirrel had to stand up all the way into Kowloon, more than an hour's ride. One of the other passengers complained to his seatmate that gasoline was so expensive that the number of buses had been cut. There were so few that the bus was crowded all the time.

He got off at the stop on Nathan Road. He found the garbage truck parked just off Nathan on Jordan Road. The keys were under the floor mat, as he'd been told they would be. The engine was loud in the early morning quiet. Only a few people were on the street, and he hoped they were all too busy with their own thoughts to notice him. He parked the truck behind another and walked up the small rise to some bushes.

He saw there wasn't much in the garbage cans; every bit of food was being used to feed the people interned. Even so, there were people going through the cans searching for anything thrown out.

He stayed in the bushes on the hillside above the fence, hidden from the camp, until a garbage truck with an open bed on the back drove into the area. He stepped out of the bushes, jumped down over the fence, and helped the worker empty the cans, as if he had arrived on the truck, also. Two men in ragged clothes mingled with the people searching the cans, then made their way over to the truck. In a flash, they were up in the truck, digging hiding places under the pile of garbage. Squirrel got in the front seat of the truck with the driver, and they drove off. At the gate, guards checked the load, but didn't stick their bayonets into the pile, as they did sometimes. Squirrel thanked God for that small miracle.

They got back to Nathan Road, drove north a while, then turned left at the base of the mountain onto Castle Peak Road, headed around the end of Lion Road Mountain to the New Territories. A Japanese patrol car pulled out of a side street right in front of the truck, and the truck hit the car. The driver jumped out of the truck.

"Listen, when it is quiet, get out of the truck and climb over the mountain to Sha Tin and the Pagoda of Ten Thousand Buddhas. That is where the guerrillas will meet you," Squirrel said to the men in the pile of garbage.

"Climb the mountain?"

"Yes, it looks steep, but is easy to climb. Once over the mountain, you can see the pagoda. I'll try to divert their attention."

He heard the sound of a gun, then saw that the Japanese officer had shot the truck driver and was motioning for him to come. He climbed down from the truck and handed the officer his residence card.

"You are policeman? Why you ride the garbage truck?" The officer, an older, heavyset man, spoke English when Squirrel didn't respond to Japanese.

"I am off duty, catching a ride."

"You at Kowloon City station?"

"Yes."

"We go there."

Squirrel was put in the backseat, and they drove off to the police station where he had worked and lived so happily. He remembered when he and the Beautiful Wife came there to live. The flat was British style, but neat and newly painted. She had walked into the big bedroom and smiled. Then when they brought 'A Fei home from the hospital, to this flat, they had walked on air. They knew by then that this would be their only child, but she was enough.

Chapter Eight

The police car pulled into the drive at 169 Boundary, and they took Squirrel to the jail cells at the back of the building. He was put in with two other men in the first one. He looked with a curled lip at the condition of the floor. *We saw the cells were cleaned every day if they were occupied, but this cell hasn't been cleaned since I left here,* he thought.

There was a bucket in the corner, but the other residents had missed the bucket most of the time. Dirt and leaves had blown in the open bars that made the front. Although sheltered by the building in front, the open bars let in every cold puff of wind passing by.

He walked to the back of the small room and spoke to the men huddled there. He recognized one as a small-time criminal that had been in that cell before. The other man identified himself as the owner of a jewelry shop in Kowloon City; he had been caught making too big a profit in money changing.

He was just behind the back door of his flat. He remembered that 'A Fei liked to play with some of the British children, and they would come to the back door to find her at times. But this was no game.

In less than an hour, a Japanese private came to escort Squirrel into the police station. Inside the door of the charge room, the private turned right and knocked on the door of what had been the AuYeung family's small parlor. An answer from inside let the private open the door and push Squirrel in.

All of their furniture had been removed from the room. Now only a gray metal desk and three chairs were there. An officer was seated at a desk at one side of the room. Squirrel was pushed to sit in a straight chair in the middle of the room. Another officer sat near the desk. The frosted windows dimmed the bright sunlight outside, but he could see scars on the floor and walls that weren't there in his time.

The officer seated at the desk, an older man with thinning hair and an angry look on his face, spoke in Japanese, and the second officer, a younger man, interpreted into Mandarin.

"The duty officer reports that it has been several weeks since you reported here at this station. What have you been doing?"

"I returned to my home village in China and visited my family."

"Why have you returned to Hong Kong?"

"There is no work in my village. I came back to try to find work here."

"How much did they pay you to help the prisoners escape from Shum Shui Po?"

"Have some prisoners escaped?"

The questioning continued; Squirrel kept his face calm and his eyes interested, but seldom answered. He thought about the Beautiful Wife and 'A Fei in this room. It was kept dusted and in order, in case any of the officers' wives should drop in.

Finally, the officer behind the desk nodded. A husky sergeant who had been standing at the back of the room moved up to Squirrel. He had not been aware of the muscular man until then. He grabbed Squirrel's arm and hauled him roughly to his feet, planting a few well-aimed blows to his body. He tied Squirrel's thumbs together behind his back, pulled him over to the doorway, and pointed at a small stool for him to stand on. Then his arms were lifted above his head and hooked on a hangar above the open door, with him facing the hall. His toes barely touched the stool. The pressure on his chest muscles made it hard to breathe unless he pushed hard against the stool. The questioning continued with few answers, and Squirrel was about to loose consciousness when someone stepped up to him in the hallway outside the room.

"Why don't you tell them what they want to know? This is a painful position."

Squirrel opened his eyes and saw that it was Capt. Shimamura. "What time is it?"

The captain looked at his watch. "Ten fifteen; why?"

The officer in charge jumped up from his chair and kicked the stool out from under Squirrel's feet. "You talk to him and won't talk to me!"

In seconds, Squirrel was unconscious.

When he came to, he had been lifted down from the hook and laid out on the floor. His face was wet, as well as the top of his jacket and shirt, where water had been used to bring him back to consciousness.

"Now, you see what we can do if you don't answer truthfully and fully the questions I ask. Did you help the men escape this morning? Where are they now?"

Squirrel wondered how long he had been unconscious. There hadn't been enough time for the two men to climb the mountain and find the pagoda. That would take at least four hours; only about three had passed by when he asked Capt. Shimamura the time. Could he hold out for another hour?

All three men were back into the room. The sergeant helped Squirrel up and sat him in the chair.

"Why did you want to know what time it was? You think you can help these men escape with more time? They will be caught and severely punished, and you with them soon."

"I did meet the men, and they hid under the garbage in the truck. But I don't know where they went after the truck stopped. I was held and brought here, but they were still in the garbage when I left. They could be anywhere around where the truck stopped. One of the men spoke some Cantonese, so they could have found a hiding place nearby."

"They are nowhere in the area. Every building has been carefully searched."

"I don't know then."

The questioning went on again. Then the officer in charge nodded once more to the sergeant standing behind Squirrel. He stood Squirrel up and began to wind rope around him until he was unable to move except for his head. Then the sergeant and the interpreter picked Squirrel up and carried him into the bathroom, putting him down into the tub with his head under the faucet. A cloth was tied over his face, and the faucet slowly turned on to drip onto the cloth. He didn't know what would happen, and his muscles tensed up. His breathing became shallow.

As soon as the cloth was saturated with water, his breathing became difficult; he was gulping down quantities of water through his nose and mouth with every breath he tried to take. He was getting less and less air, and more and more water in his lungs.

He tried to pray, "Our Father ..."

The cloth was jerked off, and the water stopped. The Japanese officer thought Squirrel was giving information, but the interpreter told him that it was merely a prayer. That made the officer angry, and he shoved Squirrel's face under the water drip again and pulled the cloth over it. Squirrel again struggled to breathe, then decided to give some information, some wrong information.

"Sha Tin," he said, and the cloth was jerked aside again. It would take at least thirty minutes to drive to Sha Tin. Of course, they could telephone a post in Sha Tin if the telephone was working.

"Sha Tin? How were they to get there? What is in that fishing village for them?"

He didn't answer, and the cloth was tied over his face again. For the third time, his face was put under the tap. He automatically struggled for breath. Then everything went black; he breathed out a long, gurgling sigh; and the struggle ceased.

The Missing Twin

Chapter One

We sat in the living room at the study table with our language teacher, a tall Chinese man named Mr. Law. Suddenly, we heard *ping*, followed by the sound of glass breaking. Then another *ping* and other glass breaking.

I got up and started down the hall, Bobbie Jo just behind me. From my bedroom on the left, the sounds came again. Opening the door, we saw broken windows and glass scattered on the floor. What was going on? We heard another *ping*, but it was outside the flat, probably the window on the landing of the stairs. Someone was shooting out our windows. Someone must be on the roof of the next building.

I grabbed the telephone and called the Business Office of our mission located Ground Floor, on the 169 side, reporting that our windows were being shot out. They promised to call the police immediately, but told us to stay away from that area.

Bobbie Jo Marston, a medical doctor, and I, Connie Osborne, a college English teacher, were brand-new to Hong Kong. We had just settled into the flat at 167 Boundary, second floor, with a third single woman, Martha Bigelow, and had started our study of the Cantonese language. Four teachers came to our flat, each for an hour every day, and we used the living room as a study room. Martha, a social worker with the many refugees, who had already finished her first-year language course, studied in the dining room, but she had gone out that morning.

The study table was about the size of a card table, and with three people's books, could be quite crowded. We put it in the southeast corner of the room, beneath the two windows that looked out onto the veranda. Our three chairs and a couch were the only other pieces of furniture in the room.

On the inside wall was a small fireplace, flanked by built-in bookcases. The upper part of the royal poinciana tree in front of the building showed over the four-foot wall around the veranda, its red blossoms, only in the treetop, just opening to their four- or five-inch size. I still had a hard time thinking that flowers bloomed in the winter here in the subtropics.

It was a cool morning, and the windows were closed. The sun was bright and by noon, the air would be warm enough to do without our sweaters, but they felt good that morning. Our teacher wore a sweater vest under his suit coat, and it was said the Chinese wear two or three layers underneath their "outside" clothes in cold weather.

We went back to our table. Mr. Law was still seated, but looking at the hall door to see what had happened. He was a man approaching middle age, his black hair slicked back with a neat part. He wore a European-style suit and carried a leather briefcase bulging with books and papers.

"We have called the office, and they will call the police," I said.

"Do you really want to call the police?" Mr. Law asked. He frowned and seemed to shrink back.

"Why, yes, why not?" Bobbie Jo asked.

"It can be a lot of bother to call the police. No one has been hurt, have they?"

"No, no one is hurt, but several windows are broken, and there is broken glass on the floor. If anyone had been in that bedroom, someone could have been hurt. Isn't that something to call the police for? We don't want him to continue to shoot at our windows."

Mr. Law said no more, but we got the impression that he'd put up with most anything rather than call the police. After a short time, he went on with the lesson. We heard no other shots, and our lesson ended soon after.

"Mr. Law, maybe you should go down the steps on the 169 side. Whoever was shooting might be watching for someone to come out from our stairway," I said. I led him through the doorway that had been cut in the wall that separated our veranda from the veranda of the flat on the 169 side, through the French door into the living room of that flat, then out the front door. Two older single women shared this flat and allowed our passage through. I knew both were at work, so it wouldn't interrupt for us to show Mr. Law out this way.

Two policemen came soon after, accompanied by the business manager, Art Burgess. They inspected the damage and reported that they had already been on the roof of the building next door and found no one. There were not even any shell casings!

"Look here." The younger policeman, in his dark blue winter uniform, knelt looking at the broken glass, then picked up something. "He was shooting marbles!" He held up a marble for us to see. Then we could see others on the floor. "He probably had a slingshot or something like that and shot at the window with it." The younger policeman, though Chinese, spoke English fluently.

The older policeman, also Chinese, spoke in Cantonese, and then the younger policeman translated. "Who lives in this room?"

"I do," I answered.

"You are an American?" once again translated.

"Yes. I have been in Hong Kong since January 10 of this year."

"May I see your passport?"

I turned to my desk, opened a drawer, took out my passport, and handed it to the older policeman, who was clearly in charge.

They looked at Bobbie Jo's passport and asked about Martha's. Then they asked to speak to the servants. All that was in Cantonese.

Finally, the conclusion was translated to us as "Probably someone had a grudge against foreigners and thought breaking some windows would make him feel better. I don't think anything more will happen, but we will watch the building next door to see if anyone does suspicious things."

The policeman seemed to think there would no other trouble. Art thought there would be no other trouble. But I was the one who lived in that room and slept in that room. I wasn't so sure that there would be no other trouble.

I slept on the living room couch that night and took a long time to go to sleep. Why had I come to Hong Kong? To teach in a refugee college, yes, but was that the real reason? Maybe I just wanted some excitement! I had a good job teaching English 101 in a junior college near my hometown. I had a nice apartment and friends. Not so many of the male variety, however. Fellows that I went to school with were either gone from this small town, as my brother was, or already married.

I thought about my brother, reported missing in Vietnam soon after my arrival in Hong Kong. My parents had been unhappy to see me leave the States for some faraway place with Jon already in Vietnam. And what had happened to Jon? The reports that my parents received and sent on to me had been sketchy. I called them when I received their cable and got them up early in the morning. We haven't learned to talk on the radiophone yet, so missed the first words every time the switch was changed.

Jon had been a field advisor in South Vietnam helping to win the loyalty of the rural people to the central government. But that unit didn't know what had happened to him. He was just gone, they said. I felt sure that he wasn't dead, even though many advisors were somehow killed after articles telling what a good job they were doing appeared in American newsmagazines or papers. Surely, a twin would know when the other had died. We had always known when important things happened to the other. So I had reassured our parents.

I thought about the broken windows. I had never had shots aimed at me or my house. I guess Jon had, but he'd never said anything about it. Even though they weren't gunshots, we didn't know that they weren't until the police came. I had felt puzzled first, then scared, then sort of exhilarated when we found out it was only marbles. Exciting, but not dangerous.

Finally, I drifted off to sleep. Sometime during the night, I came awake, hearing a loud whistling. What could be happening now? I got up, went out on the veranda, and looked over the veranda wall. I could see in the streetlights that a company of soldiers in uniform was marching up Boundary Street, and they were whistling! After listening for several moments, I recognized "Waltzing Matilda"! My guess was that it was a unit of Australian soldiers marching from the airport to the camp on Waterloo Road, about a mile away.

Quite a lot of excitement in one day for an English teacher from a small town in Missouri! I went back to bed and finally back to sleep.

Chapter 2

A couple of days later, I had a phone call from the police. "Please come to Argyle Street Police Station at 3:00 to see Inspector Brown. And bring your passport."

So at three, I appeared at the Argyle Street station, about four blocks from Boundary Street. It was cold and overcast. The wind blew out of the north, straight from Siberia it felt like. I wore my long red coat, the warmest I had, and walking helped me not to freeze.

The police station was a new, two-story, square, cement and glass building, fronting right on the sidewalk. No old Chinese decorations or gardens here.

Inspector Brown came out into the charge room to meet me. *How polite,* I thought. He was a middle-aged man, short and becoming stocky, with a wide forehead, and wearing a business suit, not a uniform.

"Please be seated. Did you bring your passport?" Inspector Brown sat behind his desk and studied my passport when I handed it to him.

"What is this about?" I asked, puzzled by his interest in the passport.

"Do you have a brother in South Vietnam?"

"How did you know?"

"We checked with the American Consulate while investigating the disturbance at your flat. I believe it was your room where the windows were broken?"

"Yes, it was. But it could have been the windows in the next room on that side, couldn't it? It wasn't because I lived in that room, was it?"

Inspector Brown didn't answer, but continued to look at my passport.

"Do you hear from your brother?" he asked.

"Hear from my brother? Of course I do, or did. I haven't heard from him since he was reported missing! We are twins, you know."

"Yes, well, thank you for your cooperation. Here is your passport."

That was all? How odd to call me down here and do nothing but study my passport and ask about Jon.

I got home in time for my four o'clock conversation class with my favorite teacher, the only woman among our four teachers. We talked simple conversation, to give me practice, an opportunity for the teacher to correct my tones, my pronunciation, and to teach me something about the culture.

I told her that I had just come from the police station. She looked at me in amazement. "You had to go to the police station? Why?"

I told her about the puzzling interview.

"My father was a policeman. He was killed by the Japanese during the occupation. I was only about six years old at the time. I know that he was a good man, a Christian, but still, he was a policeman. We Chinese fear the police and want to have as little to do with them as possible. I'm surprised that you were not afraid to go to the police station."

I remembered how Mr. Law tried to discourage us from calling the police on the day the windows were broken.

When class was over, I went down to talk to Art Burgess.

"Why would the police want to see me? And he only studied my passport and then thanked me. What is going on?"

"I don't know either. But I will call a man at the consulate that I know, and maybe he can find out," Art said.

That night was the weekly mission prayer meeting and social gathering. This meeting meant that we saw everybody in the mission every week, and it had a binding effect on us all. We became as close as or closer than we were with our blood brothers and sisters.

"I'm looking for Connie Osborne," a voice said behind me. I looked around at several new faces. There was a new accent in the voice that spoke. He was not much taller than I, sort of slouchy, but good-looking, with curly brown hair, dark brown eyes, and a smiling mouth.

"I'm Connie Osborne," I said.

"I met a man named Jon Osborne a while ago, and he said if I was ever in Hong Kong, to look you up. I'm Bryan Campbell."

"When? When did you meet Jon?"

"Oh, a while ago in Saigon," he said.

"Oh, I thought you meant recently. He's been missing for several weeks now." I was plunged to the depths.

"No, I hadn't heard that. I'm sorry. I probably built you up only to let you down. I'm really sorry," he said.

"Where are you from?" I was puzzled by the accent.

"Australia."

"Australia! I heard some Aussies go by the other night. They were whistling "Waltzing Matilda" as they marched down Boundary Street at three in the morning!"

"Huh! And I was doing some of the whistling and marching!"

"Are you in the Australian army or what?" He was dressed in a jacket and trousers, not a uniform.

"You might could say that. I'm a former student of Dr. MacGilvary, when I was at university at home in Australia. When I heard that he was teaching here since he retired, I decided to look him up, and he invited us to come with him tonight. He is speaking, I think he said."

Dr. MacGilvary came in at that time, happy as always. In the short time I had known him, he had become my friend, too. He bent his head to hear better, and the smile on his lips was in his eyes, too. He had abundant white hair and a little white goatee on his chin. The rest of his face was as smooth as a ripe mango's skin and tanned to almost the same color. He was teaching as a volunteer, at the same college where I would soon be teaching.

The meeting started then, and we settled into the folding chairs that had been set up in the large room, once the charge room of the police station, but now part of our mission office.

How had Bryan happened to meet Jon in Saigon? What was he doing in Saigon? Were the Australians advising in Vietnam now? What was he doing now in Hong Kong? Was he just 'in the army'?

Chapter Three

On Thursday, Bryan called to ask me to dinner Friday night and to talk about Jon.

To say that I was excited was the understatement of the year. In the months that we had been in Hong Kong, this was my first night out. Bobbie Jo, Martha, and I got pretty tired looking at each other and the four walls of the flat, with only the change of teachers for variety. Sometimes we saw Janet and Mary, the two older single women next door, for short conversations. Studying at home might be okay for couples with children, but for singles, we felt confined with only these other new female friends for companionship.

"What do you think you will wear?' Martha asked at our evening meal.

"Why not suggest that you go to the Marco Polo? That's such an elegant restaurant, I hear!" Bobbie Jo said.

"And be sure to take him for a ride on the Star Ferry after you eat," Martha added.

I probably changed clothes five or six times before I was satisfied with my looks. I hadn't asked Bryan how I should dress. He had worn casual clothes when he came to the meeting. He might do so again. So I decided to wear a skirt and sweater, as I would have back in the States. The problem was that I had lost some weight since my arrival in Hong Kong, so my clothes didn't fit as well as before.

When Bryan came, he wore the same pants and jacket that he had on Tuesday night. "These are the only clothes that I have besides my uniform. I hope you don't mind."

"Of course not," I said. "The first week I was here, I had only a few things to wear until all my luggage got here."

I chose a Russian place, Tschenkinko's, behind the European YMCA. I borrowed the blue Volkswagen assigned to Martha, since she would be at home all evening. I could park at the "Y," one advantage of membership!

"Why are Russians here?" Bryan asked.

"They are White Russians that fled to China during the Russian revolution after the World War I. Many of them settled in Shanghai. Now that the government in China has changed, they have fled once again, to Hong Kong. There are several Russian restaurants, as well as other types of businesses that are run by Russians."

We ate sharkslik and rice and felt sophisticated. It was almost like I was talking to Jon. Bryan didn't look or talk like Jon, but still he reminded me of Jon.

"I have gone through channels and inquired about Jon," Bryan said. "I couldn't find out anything."

"Yes, it has been very puzzling. Even the unit he was advising insists that they don't know what happened. He was just gone, they said. But I think that he is okay. We feel it when the other is in trouble."

"I hope you are right," he said.

We talked about Hong Kong since it was his first time there. I showed off my few months' experience, telling him many places he should see. I even told him about my trip to Macau, and how, on our return to Hong Kong, the British immigration officer had threatened the teenage girl with us because her parents' visa had expired. She traveled on their passport as a minor. I had been so nervous and scared that my face was red for three hours afterward.

Bryan told me about some of his other assignments. We talked and laughed until the place was almost empty. Then we rode the Star Ferry to the Hong Kong side and back. I was glad that he had met Jon and Jon had asked him to look me up.

On Monday, Art Burgess, our business manager, called to set up an appointment for me with his friend from the American Consulate. My free hour from language study was at three, so at that time I went downstairs to the office.

Art took me to one of the small meeting rooms, furnished with only a small table and four chairs. The one window was glazed. Outside, the light was shadowy since the room was on the ground floor and the trees and plants shaded it. Inside was dimmer still, so I switched on the light. The room smelled of dust and mold.

Then Art went down the hall to the back door and let a man in from outside. Why didn't he come in through the main office? He was a tall man, thin and middle-aged, with a few long strands of black hair combed over his bald head.

"This is George Bradley. I know him because he comes to the English-language church where I go. He has some information for you, Connie," Art said.

We sat down at the table. Mr. Bradley took some papers out of his briefcase and spread them out on the table. I could see that they were maps.

"This is a map showing where Jon was when he disappeared, not far from Dalat, near New Town, being built to resettle people from the country villages. The area was heavily infested with communist guerillas, but with Jon's help, the local guard commander and district commissioner were winning the loyalty of the people." He spoke in a harsh, nasal voice.

"It may be that Jon was kidnapped as they walked single file along a narrow road in the mountains. He just disappeared. No trace was found. That is about all I can tell you at this time. We are still working to find out what happened," he said. He looked into my eyes for the first time. I felt that he was truly concerned for Jon, and sorry to have so little information for me.

Mr. Bradley folded up his maps and soon left, once again by the back door. Why was this?

I tried to concentrate for the next several days. Our six-month language exams were coming up, and I spent many hours with my tape recorder, listening and trying to imitate the sounds that I heard. I walked along the streets every afternoon for some exercise. Traffic was always heavy, and the exhaust fumes filled the air. I liked the wind, even though it was often piercingly cold; at least it cleared the air for a moment.

Bryan came to dinner once, still wearing the jacket and trousers that he wore the first time I saw him. I went with him to a movie once and talked to him on the phone several times. Then one night late, he called.

"I just wanted to say good-bye. I'm being sent on another assignment. I'm glad that I met Jon Osborne in Saigon and that he asked me to look you up. It's been great!"

I was without words. Then I said, "Yes, it has been great. I'm glad that you looked me up. Will you come back to Hong Kong?"

"I don't know, but if I do, you may be sure I'll be in touch."

I was surprised to find everything seemed flat after Bryan left. I had just seen him four times and talked on the phone five or six, so why was it that the days were tasteless and dry when I knew he was gone?

The day of our exam came. One of the older missionaries, who spoke Cantonese well, came to give the oral exam. We all sat in our living room. He spoke to us in simple sentences and asked easy questions. Why couldn't we understand him? We had gone over those same questions and answers many times with our teachers. After he repeated the questions several times, one of us would catch on and answer. I felt some moisture break out on my forehead, and looking at Bobbie Jo, I saw that she was wiping her moist hands. Finally, the examiner seemed satisfied that we were learning at the normal speed.

Our teacher told us later that everyone has a bit of an accent depending on where and when he or she learned Cantonese, as it is only a spoken language.

We had a couple of days' vacation, so we decided to go to Cheung Chau Island overnight. It was about an hour's ferry ride from the Hong Kong side. For a hundred years a vacation spot for foreigners living in China, it was called the "dumbbell island" because of its shape, two round pieces with hilly tops connected by a narrow neck. All five of the singles went. We stayed in a flat owned by another mission and used as a vacation flat. By splitting the rent, we could afford it.

"What is there to do?" I asked. "It's not warm yet, so no swimming."

"We can hike over the high middle of the big island and look around in the few shops. There are no cars and no roads, just cement walkways here and there. There's only one telephone on the island, and that's in the general store on the waterfront," Janet, one of the older women, said.

"We can look into the pirates' cave and go to see the floats and racks where the white steamed buns are lined up during the Bun Festival in May," Mary, the other one, said.

The exercise made me sleep well that night, and I got up late the next morning. I was eager to go back and buckle down to another semester of language study.

Chapter Four

On the ferry coming back from Cheung Chau, I began to have an uneasy feeling about Jon. I had reassured our parents, and myself, that Jon wasn't in serious trouble or I would have felt it. Now, I felt a growing restlessness.

Please keep Jon safe. Tell me if there is something I should do.

The wind was strong enough that the canvas awnings on the ferry had been lowered and tied to protect the passengers. The canvas snapped and occasionally popped. People were eating from twists of paper, spitting out the husks of sunflower seeds, reading the paper, sleeping, or talking with friends. My four companions were mostly quiet. I couldn't sit quietly, but got up and walked from one end of the seating area to the other, at times lurching with the roll of the ferry.

"Connie, what's wrong?" Bobbie Jo asked as I passed the bench where they were seated. No one was on the bench just in front of them, so I switched the back of that bench and sat down facing my friends.

"I don't know, but I can't be quiet. I have to move." I was up and walking down the central aisle before anything else was said.

I passed my friends again. "I'm beginning to think that something is seriously wrong with Jon," I said. Another round, and I threw myself down on the bench facing them. "I don't know what to do." And I was up walking again.

At the ferry pier on the Hong Kong side, we took the Star Ferry back to the Kowloon side and caught the bus to Boundary Street.

I had a serious conversation with God that night as I knelt by my bed in robe and pajamas. After a time with my face down on the bed, I began to feel some relief. There was still danger, but something was already underway to handle it.

All through Sunday, I still felt uneasy, but taught the twenty-third psalm to my Bible study class (in English at the Mandarin-speaking church). I felt some comfort from the study myself.

We ate lunch at the Ambassador Hotel, whose dining room on the top floor looks out over the harbor. But I didn't see much that day.

I was up early on Monday morning. Mondays and Thursdays, from five to seven o'clock, were our two water days. We were all up and took baths while the cook filled the big galvanized containers in the kitchen. I don't know when she got up and filled the barrel-shaped electric water heater in the bathroom, but there was hot water for us to dip into the tub. When baths were finished, the bathtub was cleaned and filled with water. We laughed at the report in the newspaper from a British water expert that Hong Kong received enough water from typhoon rains to need no more reservoirs. What happened when the typhoons were dry? Fresh water had been a problem since the early days, and when a flood of refugees pushed in, it had come to this severe rationing.

After breakfast, of toast and coffee for me, I hunted up the card George Bradley had given me and called him as soon as the office opened at nine.

"Mr. Bradley, I've begun to worry about Jon. Have you heard anything more?"

"No, I haven't heard anything, but I will check my sources and get back to you," he said.

My mind was not really on the Cantonese language during the day. I kept waiting for the phone to ring. Then my last class was over, and still no call. It was too late to call the consulate again. I went out and walked along the street for almost an hour, but the exercise didn't quiet my jumpiness.

That night I dreamed about Jon and me when we were growing up. But then my dream turned weird. We were yelling at each other, just about to land some blows, when I awoke. I couldn't remember the words we were yelling, and I didn't know what the fight was about.

I called Mr. Bradley again on Tuesday morning.

"I'm sorry, Miss Osborne. I can't find out anything more at this time," he said. I wished that Bryan were still in Hong Kong. I could talk to him about Jon, and even though he couldn't resolve my apprehension, it would help just to talk to him.

It was almost a week later that Mr. Bradley called me.

"Miss Osborne, could you come to the consulate sometime today? Speak to Art Burgess about it."

"Let me see if I can get out of class this afternoon. I'll call you back as soon as I can arrange it."

I talked to Art Burgess, and he told me how to cancel classes that afternoon. Since Bobbie Jo and I studied together, the teachers wouldn't teach just one of us, so the classes had to be canceled. Bobbie Jo was glad for an unexpected afternoon off.

I caught a bus to the Star Ferry and crossed the mile-wide harbor. The water reflected the clear blue of the sky. The sun warmed me and made me think that hot, humid summer days were not far away.

The harbor was crowded with other ferries, sampans used as water taxis, junks with high sterns and patched sails gliding through, a passenger liner tied up at the Ocean Terminal, and in the distance a US Navy aircraft carrier from the Gulf of Tonkin in for R and R. Sometimes a craft would blow its horn to warn another, but the ferry motor covered other sounds.

On the Hong Kong side, I took a taxi up the steep hill past Government House and the Botanical Gardens to the American Consulate, a cream-colored utilitarian rectangle with the US seal on the front.

As I got out of the taxi, I looked on the opposite side of the street at the lower terminal of the Peak Tram. I wished I had time to ride up to the peak. On such a clear day, surely I could see all the way to Vietnam.

Mr. Bradley was waiting for me in the lobby and led me to a third-floor office with no name on the door. Two men were already in the office. One was a young Asian man; the other an older man, with a stomach that hung over his belt and a receding hairline. They both stood up as we entered the office. Although there were no windows, the room was well lit by the fluorescent fixture, and bare except for a small table and four chairs around it.

"This is Henry Brown and Nuygen Yan Fat," Mr. Bradley said as he indicated each man with his hand. "Let's sit down and talk about a project we have in mind."

"How much taller than you is your brother?" the older man asked.

"Jon is about two inches taller than I. Of course, my hair isn't slicked down like Jon's usually is, so most people think we are the same height."

"But you are thinner than Jon," Mr. Brown continued.

"Well, yes, and shaped differently," I laughed.

"What do you think, Nuygen?" Mr. Brown asked.

"The hair is the same color. That bright blond hair is what they would see. It would have to be cut shorter. Most Vietnamese think Westerners all look alike anyway, so they wouldn't notice small differences," he replied.

"What is this all about?" I asked.

"George, you want to explain?" Mr. Brown said.

"Miss Osborne, the problem is this. We can't find where Jon is being held. We think the guerrillas kidnapped him, and we've made several small raids but haven't found him. We wondered if you would be willing to help us."

"Of course, if I can."

"We had the idea that since you look so much like Jon, that perhaps you could appear as Jon at an important meeting in Dalat. That would confuse the guerillas, who would hear that Jon was at the meeting. Perhaps they would then check on Jon, and we could track them to where Jon is being held. Then a small raid could rescue Jon."

I shook my head. This was going too fast for me to really understand. "Would you go over that again?" I asked.

Mr. Bradley repeated the plan in his harsh, nasal voice. Of course, Jon and I had confused our teachers and sometimes our friends when we were younger by pretending to be the other. I could even make my voice a little deeper to sound like Jon's. But could I pull it off now?

We discussed some more about details. I couldn't just disappear without an explanation. Perhaps it wouldn't be more than a week. I would need to learn a few words in Vietnamese since Jon spoke it fluently.

"You will learn Vietnamese very quickly. You already know some Chinese," Nuygen Yan Fat said.

George Bradley laid out a plan for me to go to Saigon and no one would be the wiser. I agreed.

Chapter Five

On the way back to Boundary Street that afternoon, I stopped at the beauty salon a few blocks from 169. I had my hair cut short, shingled in the back so it looked like Jon usually wore his hair. That created a lot of comment when I got back to the flat.

"Your hair is so short."

"Your beautiful hair. How could you do this?"

"I like it," was my answer to all, even the cook.

The next day, Wednesday, I received a cablegram from my father. "Come home. Your mother needs you."

He didn't say what the matter was with Mother. I knew this was part of George Bradley's plan, but I had to act as if it were a shock to me.

Art Burgess immediately helped me make arrangements for a flight to Kansas City. This was to be at my expense and I would have to repay the mission, but it was going to be worth it. My passport and shot record were up-to-date, so no problem there.

I left on Thursday morning at seven o'clock, with the first stop to be in Taipei. I wore a dark blue skirt and my favorite pink camp shirt, embroidered across the back with a bunch of pink roses and a single rose on the left front.

I studied a Vietnamese phrase book as I ate my breakfast on the plane. I was glad that the attendant was able to find the last English breakfast of eggs and bacon in first class for me; otherwise, I would have had the Chinese breakfast of *chuk* and tea.

In Taipei after the hour's flight, I went immediately to the Cathay Pacific counter to check the schedule for Saigon. I would have several hours to wait.

I looked around in the gift shop at the souvenirs. They had some brass lamps that I really liked, and the price was low enough for me to afford them. But I couldn't be carrying around two lamps in Saigon. So I drifted off to a quiet corner of the in-transit waiting room, where I could study the phrase book. The room had a high ceiling and windows on one side, and no color except for rows of bright orange chairs filling the floor.

It was wonderful that Vietnamese had an alphabet. That was one kind thing the French did for Vietnam. They had used Chinese characters to write before the French took over. Now, I could read the words and have a good idea of how to say them.

I had studied for an hour or so when I stood up to stretch my legs. I noticed a Chinese man with a large tote bag sitting nearby. The bag was almost exactly like the one I carried, but mine was nearly full of wadded up newspaper, with a layer of my reading material on top. I walked away and bought a soft drink. When I returned to my seat, the man was gone, so I picked up the tote bag and walked to the rest room.

Once in a stall, I dug into the tote bag. Under the two magazines were clothes that would make me look like Jon. First I picked up the wide strip of cloth that I would use to flatten my breasts. I was well endowed in this area, and I didn't know if it would work and still be comfortable enough for me to wear it constantly.

I tied it around my person, and then got into the pants and shirt, which did look like something Jon would wear. Socks and shoes completed the outfit. In the bottom of the tote bag, I found a briefcase that would take the place of my purse. And in the briefcase I found a new passport with Jon's picture and a ticket to Saigon.

I put my clothes, shoes, and purse into the tote bag. I waited until there was no one else in the rest room, then put the tote bag in the bottom of the trash can, digging under a pile of used paper towels. I hated the thought that I would never see my favorite blouse again. But I could always buy another blouse, and I couldn't buy another twin.

I fluffed up my hair so I would look like a girl who had changed into more comfortable traveling clothes. I didn't want the change to be so much that I would attract attention, particularly if I met someone coming out of the ladies' rest room. Then I went to the Cathay Pacific counter to check in and get a boarding pass. They looked at the passport, then at my face, but they asked no questions. They didn't see the moisture on my face as I waited.

I returned to the waiting room, but to a different corner than before. I began reading a newspaper, holding it to cover my face more or less. Mentally, I was saying the phrases for greetings over and over.

When the Cathay Pacific flight to Saigon was called, I found a place near the end of the line waiting to board.

This flight was about two hours, as it was direct to Saigon. I slept most of the way. The attendant woke me, and I gathered up my things. I had taken all makeup off my face, and now I combed my hair in the way that Jon did. I pulled out the cloth cap with a stitched visor like Jon wore and put it on my head.

I walked down the rolling stairs from the plane onto the small paved area in front of the terminal. The air was hot and humid, and smelled of the gas fumes from the half-dozen planes on the crowded tarmac.

I walked into the terminal carrying my briefcase and wearing the cap pulled down over my eyes. The terminal was a long, wooden building. Inside I found that it was narrow, only about twenty feet wide, with arrivals at one end and departures at the other. I followed the baggage signs and waited.

"Wonder where my bag is," I mumbled aloud when most of the bags were gone from the two-level wagon. A Vietnamese man stepped up, picked up a bag, and said, "This is your bag, isn't it, Jon?"

"Oh, oh, I guess it is. I don't know where my mind was not to recognize it."

I should have known that my suitcase packed in Hong Kong with my skirts and blouses wouldn't be here. "They" were taking care of me, and so far all the details were right.

"The jeep is out this way," the same man said, and I followed him out of the terminal. I noticed then that two others were following, too. I looked sort of sideways and stopped short.

"Bryan? Bryan, is that you?"

"Sir, I think you are confused. My name is Rob Holt. We met just before you had to leave. I must look like someone you know."

No Australian accent. A different name. In an American army uniform. Even a different posture, so that he seemed to tower over me. Then I saw a quick smile. It was the man I knew as Bryan.

"I guess so." I got into the jeep and put the briefcase between my legs. The bag would go in the back with the two men.

"My name is Nuygen Thai Ming. You call me Thai. I'm your right-hand man. I will do all I can to keep you from making a mistake. Can you manage some greetings in Vietnamese?" The man driving was talking quietly as we drove along the wide boulevard with no lines to show traffic lanes. The tall banyan trees along the road shaded the street, but the smell of fumes and noise from the few cars and many motor scooters filled the air.

I repeated the greetings that I had been studying. He corrected some pronunciation.

"You'll do. These people don't know you well. They won't know how well you speak Vietnamese," Thai said.

"The conference is being held in the conference center in Dalat. We have rooms for the night here at a hotel. We'll go there now and check in. In the morning, we will fly to Dalat," Rob said from the backseat.

"Why can't we go on to Dalat today? Surely there is a late afternoon plane, or couldn't we just drive?" I asked.

For a moment, no one answered. Then Thai leaned over to talk quietly to me. "Because it is not safe to drive between cities, day or night. Because the airport at Dalat is twenty miles out of town, and it is not safe to drive to the airport at night. And do not ask such questions if you don't want to ruin the whole thing and get Jon killed." He spoke between clenched teeth and with considerable force.

"Okay, okay. I'm sorry," I said.

Thai took care of the checking in. We were put into two rooms, the three men in one room, with me in the other. Thai unlocked the connecting door, then closed it.

"We won't use this door unless it becomes necessary," Thai said as he went out.

Dalat, I thought. *That's close to where Jon was last seen.*

Chapter Six

We were on the twenty-passenger plane when it left for Dalat at 7:00 a.m. I had just sat down when I recognized the family coming down the aisle, a couple and five children, the Longs. They had stayed in Hong Kong for several weeks waiting for a visa to work as missionaries in Vietnam. Would they recognize me?

I jerked my face around to the window. Then I thought, they wouldn't know Jon. I knew them in Hong Kong, and Jon had not visited me there. They won't think it strange to see someone similar to me in looks, just a coincidence. So I tried to relax and act natural.

The oldest son had two broken arms, set so that they hung almost straight, with a slight bend at each elbow. The casts looked like a pair of parentheses hanging from his shoulders. I wondered what had happened. The house where they lived in Saigon was near enough to the presidential palace that when the guerillas shelled the palace, the shells went right over their house. Surely, their house hadn't been hit. I would have heard about it in Hong Kong. I guess they were having a few cool days of vacation.

I looked out of the window at the green land below me. It seemed peaceful and prosperous from above.

We landed at Dalat in just under an hour. The sun was bright as we walked from the plane to a waiting car, and the air was clear, cool, and dry. The humidity that wrapped around us in Saigon was gone. I remembered when I was still at home in Missouri, we would drive to Colorado to visit my grandparents. The humidity would gradually let go as we drove into drier and drier air. I felt the same freedom here in Dalat.

There was little traffic on the paved, two-lane road. There seemed to be nothing dangerous now. Why was it so different at night?

But I didn't dare ask such questions.

Dalat used to be the summer capital, I had read. The climate of the mountains was so nice after the heat of Saigon, and yet so close by. So I was surprised to see only small shops and narrow streets. It was all built on the side of a mountain, so the streets sloped this way and that. Probably that was why the airport was twenty miles out of town; it was that far to enough level ground.

The lushness of Saigon had thinned out to a few pine trees along the fencerows and the road's shoulders.

We drove through town, then on toward New Town.

"This gate is the entrance to New Town. The signboard over the gate says that," Thai broke the silence. "This is an effort of the government to provide a safe place for the rural people to live."

"How have the people responded?" I asked.

"Reluctantly," Thai answered. "They hate to leave their homes. The guerillas attack at night usually. They work their fields safely during the day. They want their small villages to be safe as well."

"The meeting today is with the leaders of the villages in the surrounding area." Rob spoke for the first time since we left Saigon. "Thai and others will try to convince them that they can come to New Town at night and still work their own fields by day. It is not that far from their home villages."

"I don't have to say anything, do I?" I asked.

"No. At times I might lean over like I was asking you something. But you don't need to say anything aloud. We will all be right beside you all the time."

Thai parked the car near a rustic building larger than the nearby houses. The yard was clean and the grass clipped. A few bright flowers grew in a small rock-bordered plot.

We walked up the gravel path. I tried to walk with Jon's particular stride. The air was clean and the sun bright. I thought again of Colorado weather. There were only a few tall pine trees. The land was flatter than in town and seemed to all be in cultivation.

Inside the wooden building, the framework and rafters were exposed. That meant no insulation, even though nights could be cold here. A fireplace in the center of a long wall had been cleaned but still had traces of ashes from last night's fire. A long table with chairs showed where the group was to gather. I followed Thai to chairs on one side of the table.

I must not react in a way that would give anyone ideas that I was not Jon. I pulled off the cloth cap and laid it on the table. I smoothed down my hair with my hand. But my stomach was all knotted up, and my breathing was shallow.

The men trickled in one at a time. They talked some among themselves, but just bowed slightly to Thai and me. Rob and Minh were out by the car.

After a time, when most of the chairs had filled up, an older man began talking to the group. He talked for several minutes, then looked at us and said something. Thai answered. He leaned over as if to say something to me, then started talking to the group. He got up and drew a map of sorts on a blackboard, then talked some more. There were questions from the group, which Thai seemed to answer easily.

When the meeting broke up, several men came up and shook hands with Thai and me. I was able to say some greeting words. One man spoke to me in English, and I smiled and spoke a greeting back in Vietnamese. This business of honoring the other by speaking in his language was sometimes difficult.

Thai spoke to the older man, who seemed to be the leader. They continued talking as we walked outside to the car. Rob and Minh opened the car door, and we got in. We waved to the old man as the car moved off.

"How did it go?" Rob asked.

"I think we pulled it off," Thai said. "Jon never said much at meetings like this. He always let me do the talking."

I felt that I might faint. My face was red; I know because I could feel the heat. My stomach heaved suddenly.

Rob must have noticed something because he turned around from the front seat and looked at me. "Do you want a drink of water?" he asked.

"Yes, I do." I hadn't noticed how dry my mouth was until then.

He pulled out a bottle of water from a bag that was on the floor. I opened the bottle and drank, stopped to breathe, and drank again.

"Now," Thai started, "we have to get you out of here and back to your own life."

In town we checked into the hotel. I once again saw the Longs with all five children. They were getting on their bikes that they had carried on the plane to ride around town. The father had rented a double bike for himself and the boy with the broken arms, and the mother had the youngest as a passenger on her bike. I ducked into the lobby, then hurried to my room.

The next morning early, we put our bags into the trunk of the car. But Rob was not there.

"Where is Rob?" I asked.

"He had something he had to do. He will see you in Saigon," Thai said.

We headed out of Dalat on the road to the airport. After we had gone about halfway, we came to some narrow curves. As we rounded one, we saw a barrier like a long sawhorse set up on the road. We had to slow down and finally come to a stop. Thai was out in a flash to move the obstacle. Before he got there, men in loose, black "pajama" outfits with guns were swarming out of the brush on the sides of the road.

"Lift backseat and get under into the trunk," Minh said quietly.

I had been slumped down resting when we stopped. Now, without raising my head, I did as Minh said and crawled under the seat, pulled the seat down over me, and then I was in the trunk.

I heard shots. I prayed for Thai and for Minh. I didn't know who was shooting and who might have been hit. Then the car was shooting forward, the horn blowing. I felt the car slow a bit, and then a door slammed. I heard tires burst in the rain of bullets, but the car continued bumping along.

Then I heard the shots stop. *Good,* I thought. But we were going so slowly that I felt the guerillas could catch us by walking fast. The inside of the trunk was dark, but I felt the pile of our bags just inside the trunk. A final shot *twanged* in the trunk lid, then a *squish* made me think the bullet was buried in the baggage. *Am I going to die here in the dark?* I felt the car turn a corner, and in a few minutes stop. I stayed where I was.

I heard men talking, and soon Minh opened the trunk.

"What happened? Is Thai all right?" I asked.

"He was hit, but I think he okay. He jumped in car when I slowed. We are at zoo. I will get help. You please put on girl's clothes from bag. Hurry."

Minh lowered the trunk lid but didn't latch it. There was enough light for me to open bags until I found a few girl's clothes in one. I was glad that I had learned to dress under the covers in my chilly bedroom before my parents got central heat. I wiggled around in the trunk to get into the blouse and skirt, then stepped out of the trunk. Pulling and twisting, I straightened my clothes and put on the sandals that I found in the bag. There was a small bag like a purse. I emptied the briefcase with my passport and shot record into the bag and found a comb. I worked on my hair, then found my lipstick.

Something was coming up the drive. I turned and saw an armored personnel carrier pull in and stop. I jumped up to where Thai was lying back on the front seat. His shirt was bloody, but one hand was holding a square of cloth on the wound in his chest. His face was white and his eyes closed.

I looked at the car. It had a line of bullet holes all around the car, as if they wanted to kill everyone who might be in it. But there was only one hole in the trunk.

The men in uniforms poured out of the carrier and inspected the line of holes in the car. Minh went up to the men, and they began all talking at once in Vietnamese. I could understand nothing.

They helped Thai out of the car and supported him as he walked into the building.

"These Home Guard. They behind us on the road. When the guerillas saw them, they went back into the brush. So we got away. Home Guard take you on to airport soon. Come into building. You do good." Minh followed the other men.

I saw blood on Minh's pants. He must have been shot also.

"We radio for helicopter to take Thai to hospital," Minh said.

While we waited, one of the zoo men offered to show me around the zoo. I hated to leave Thai and Minh, but Minh waved me on. The zoo was built on terraces, with cages on each level. We looked at the waterfall and the picnic area. After a time, I felt sick. I wasn't seeing the animals, but the guerillas on the road. I felt a bead of nervous sweat run down my jawbone. I leaned on the fence, then threw up. The zoo man was nervous that the foreigner had gotten sick. He hurried me back to the building where Thai and Minh were.

"I'm okay," I kept saying. "It has just been too scary this morning. I'll be fine in a few minutes."

In the rest room, I washed my face and ran the cold water over my wrists. Then back in the room with Thai and Minh, I sat down and closed my eyes.

Chapter Seven

Soon we heard the *whop, whop* of the helicopter coming to pick up Thai and take him to a hospital. With a great swirl of flying debris, it set down in the parking lot. They brought in a stretcher for Thai, loaded both Thai and Minh, and took off.

I felt lonely watching the helicopter growing smaller and smaller in the sky. My adventure was about over, and I would be going back to my life in Hong Kong. It seemed so dull and flat now.

The men in the personnel carrier made room for me and my bag, and we went on to the airport. I had missed the early flight and had to wait for the evening one. I thanked the men and checked in at the counter.

There were no English reading materials to be found in the small, one-room terminal. I found a seat near the boarding gate, sat down, and began to think about the past two days.

Did I fool anyone? Could everyone see through the charade? I felt let down and a complete failure. Miserable, I leaned back and closed my eyes. I could see the faces of the men at New Town. Maybe they were convinced that I was Jon. At least, they didn't openly oppose Thai and his suggestions. Then the black-clad guerillas came up on my mind's screen, and I could hear the guns again. Thai's bloody shirt and white face stayed on that screen a long time.

"Miss, Miss," someone was shaking me. I must have fallen asleep. They had called the plane, and several were lined up to board. I jumped up and collected my few belongings and joined the line.

It was nearly dark when we landed in Saigon. I went to the Cathay Pacific counter to check on flights. All would stop in Hong Kong before proceeding to the States. What if I saw someone I knew?

I went to the baggage claim wagon. I remembered when I was here last and Thai and Minh met me. Also, that character Rob. Was he really Bryan?

I found the bag, picked it up, and felt something on the padded handle. Looking at it and feeling it, I realized that it was the bullet that hit the trunk lid. I took a deep breath, thankful that I hadn't been hurt. Perhaps the guerillas knew I was in the trunk. I turned around to see a tall American man just behind me. He wore a tan, short-sleeved sport shirt and brown pants, with a smile on his tanned face.

"Miss Osborne? I'm Tom Wagner, from the embassy. I understand you had quite a time today," he said.

"Yes, I did." My voice sounded more wobbly than I felt; then I showed him the bullet.

"I'll take you to a hotel for the night, and I'll try to get that bullet out. Do you have your flight for tomorrow worked out?"

"Yes, the plane leaves at ten. I will have to change planes in Hong Kong. I'm afraid I will see someone I know; that would mess everything up."

"You'll stay in the transit room. Maybe that will help avoid seeing anyone," he said.

"Oh, that's right. I forgot."

We got in his car and drove along the wide streets to a hotel, actually the same one that we had stayed in the night before last. It didn't seem possible that so much had happened in just two days. I would have been already on the way to the States if we hadn't been attacked by the guerillas. Would I make the trip in a week as we planned?

Near the hotel, we passed a brass market, still busy and well-lighted from the string of bare lightbulbs around the stall. I remembered the brass lamps that I saw in Taipei. I wished I could find some more; they would be evidence that this detour did happen. My schedule now had me missing Taipei and changing planes in Tokyo.

"Do you know where Rob is? He left us in Dalat, and Thai said he would be here in Saigon. And how is Thai?" I asked.

"No, I don't know where Rob is at the moment. Thai was in surgery the last I heard, but they think he will be okay."

I had no more than checked into the hotel and reached my room when I heard the *harumph* of heavy gunfire. The guerillas were shelling the presidential palace again. No wonder the Longs had gotten tired of sheltering under their dining room table when the shelling started. I would take a break and go to Dalat, too. The firing wasn't close to the hotel, so I tried to ignore it.

Sleep tried to elude me that night. When I did drift off, I dreamed of black-clad men shooting guns or of Thai's white face and the bloodstained cloth he held over his wound.

I was up early and looked out my window. I could see that the stalls along the street were still covered with canvas. They had been open until late the night before. So it would be too early for the brass market to be open.

People were walking slowly along the sidewalk enjoying the coolness of the morning. Some were practicing tai chi in a small park down the street.

The car from the embassy finally came to take me to the airport. Still no word from Rob. Maybe he'd be at the airport.

A man was taking down the canvas coverings from the stall that sold brass when we drove past. I got the driver to stop after a lot of talking. He didn't really understand English, and my Vietnamese was limited to greetings. But he got the idea, turned around, and drove back to the market.

I found two large candle stands that I thought I could get wired as lamps, so bought them. The man in the stall tied them together with a piece of heavy twine, and I set off with them carried in one hand, clanging together.

I checked in at the Cathay Pacific counter and checked my bag, but carried the brass lamps with me. I walked around the terminal. Surely Rob would be here. Up on the mezzanine was an eating place. I took a turn around that area.

But there was no Rob. I hung around and watched the people. I heard the flight called, but still I looked for him. Finally, the last call for that flight came over the speakers. I made my way slowly to the small counter and presented my boarding pass. The attendant's eyes opened wide. Her mouth moved as she lifted the walk-through in the counter. "Through here," she said and pointed to a door in the back of the small space. "You need to walk past the Pan Am plane that is parked, turn to the left in front of the Air France plane, then over to the Cathay Pacific. And hurry."

I jogged as fast as I could, with the lamps clanging every step, holding my boarding pass plus the bag I used as a purse in the other hand. Sweat popped out on my forehead in the morning heat. Past the Pan Am plane, I turned left and saw the rolling stairs moving away from the Cathay Pacific plane. The men stopped when they saw me coming and replaced the stairs. The door of the plane was closed, and I knocked as soon as I got to the top of the stairs. The flight attendants opened the door and stared at me, then at the boarding pass and the brass lamps.

"Just a minute," one of the attendants said and checked his list. "I'll have to put you in first class. Economy is full."

I walked into first class and began to settle in the only empty seat, one on the aisle. The attendant helped me put the lamps in the overhead compartment, then I sat down.

"I thought you weren't going to make it," the man in the window seat reading a newspaper said.

"Rob, Bryan, whatever your name is, I looked all over the terminal for you." I managed a short laugh, but felt the tears gather in my eyes.

"I know that you've had a lot of surprises in the last few hours, but this is my only opportunity to see you for a while. I wanted to say some things to you. The plane will stop in Phnom Pen. I must leave you then. Can you bear some more now?"

I leaned my head on his shoulder and tried to stop crying. His arm was around me, and his head leaned down on mine. I drew a long breath and fumbled for a handkerchief. He offered me his, and I mopped my face and eyes.

Finally, I raised my head and looked at him. "What do you want to tell me?"

"Some explanations. When I heard that Jon had been captured and even the raids couldn't find him, I remembered that he had often spoken of you in Hong Kong. But I didn't know if you could handle doing what was required to carry this off. First, I broke your windows with marbles.

"You did that?"

"Yes, I did. I knew the police would be called and that they would run your name past the consulate. The consulate people asked the local police to see you and assess the possibility of your acting as Jon. Then I checked you out myself. George Bradley got involved. He's a good man, but in a delicate position. He took risks, but brought you to the consulate to see the others."

I looked at Bryan/Rob. He had arranged it all. Who was he anyway? Must not be an Australian. He wasn't in uniform today, but he had been yesterday.

"Who are you? You are not the Bryan that I liked and trusted. Are you Rob, all business? How could you arrange all this?"

"Connie, I understand this has been a strange experience for you. All I wanted was to work out some way to find Jon. We need him. I thought I could protect you by being with the group from Saigon to Dalat. Somehow the personnel carrier got delayed, and that let the guerillas attack your car as Thai and Minh took you to the airport. I was sick when I heard what had happened. I'm glad that you weren't hurt."

"Yes, well, Minh told me to get under the backseat and roll into the trunk. I don't think the guerillas even saw me. But Thai was hit in the chest and was bleeding a lot. I keep seeing his face when I close my eyes."

He tightened his arm around me. I wanted to relax and let him take care of everything.

"How will I know if you can find Jon?" I had my composure in hand and straightened up.

"I'll let you know; never fear," Bryan/Rob said.

Just then, the attendant announced our approach to Phnom Pen.

"I won't be able to talk to you in the terminal, so I'll say good-bye now. I'll be in touch whenever I can," he said.

He was the first one off the plane. The attendant insisted that everyone must go into the in-transit room, so I dragged out. I looked at the small case of souvenirs, but they wouldn't take Vietnamese or Hong Kong money. I had only a few US dollars, and I would need them when I got to the States. Oh, well, I didn't need more junk. I had the brass lamps as evidence of my time here anyway.

Chapter Eight

My flight to the States was uneventful. I saw no one I knew during the layover in Hong Kong, so I began to relax. I called my parents from the last change in Chicago, and they got to the airport in Kansas City just as my plane landed.

"Connie, is something wrong? Have you bad news about Jon?" My mother frowned in worry as she threw her arms around me. I was surprised to see that she had more gray hair than when I left about six months before.

"Yes, Connie, we're glad to see you, but what is this all about?" My Dad hugged me to him. His shoulders were bent a little more, and his sideburns were all white.

"I'll explain as soon as we are in the car, but still no news about Jon," I said.

We drove the fifty miles home, and I talked most of the way. I told them about the windows being broken out, the interviews with the police and George Bradley, and the visit to the consulate. I kept cautioning them to mention the situation to no one. I told about my trip to Vietnam and how I passed as Jon. But I didn't tell them about being shot at and how Thai looked so pale and bloody. They would not be able to bear that bit of news.

My mother's face was tired and worn, as if she had been in Vietnam with me. My dad was solemn as the car turned into our drive.

I didn't intend to see any friends, but if I did, I'd say that I had a chance to come on a special deal and couldn't pass it up. My parents could give the same answer to anyone asking questions.

I stayed three days with my parents, glad to see them but not feeling at home as I once had, then flew back to Hong Kong. I got a taxi at the airport and arrived at 169 Boundary without telling anyone my schedule. The aromas of the air identified Hong Kong loud and clear as I rode along in the car.

The flat looked so new and strange, as if I had never lived here before, yet nothing had changed. I was the one who was different, with all that happened since I left just days before. Still, I knew that my life was here now, not back in Missouri with my parents. I'd probably be less homesick than before.

Martha and Bobbie Jo were a little stiff with surprise, but soon loosened up, asking me questions about the trip and my parents. They wanted to know everything. I told them as much as I could without mentioning my days in Vietnam, and I think I satisfied them.

I had one day to rest, and then, back to language study with Bobbie Jo.

The time in Vietnam receded until it was like a dream. Did it really happen, or was it my imagination? I couldn't talk it over with anyone to remind myself of the terror of being shot at or the horror of seeing Thai pale and bloody or the thrill of seeing Bryan again. My hair began to grow out. I had left the brass lamps-to-be in Missouri with my parents, and I bought another camp shirt like the one I left in Taipei airport, only this one was white with red roses.

In June, an early typhoon, the first for Bobbie Jo and me, was forecast to be swiping Hong Kong within a couple of days. The weather was hot and sticky, and the winds picked up until the number five ball was hoisted on Observatory Hill. From the years before there were radios, severity of typhoons was announced by hanging different shaped wicker balls, five feet in height, from a high point on Observatory Hill on the Kowloon side. Everything stopped—ferries first, then buses, and schools, businesses, and other gatherings all closed when the number eight ball went up.

The wind was scary, but it was straight wind, not the funnel clouds that we worried about in Missouri.

"We are in no danger. All lines—power, telephone, and any other—are all buried underground," Mary, our neighbor, reassured us as all five of us ate together that evening in our flat. "The power will not go out, and we can talk to anyone on the phone."

"Just stay inside. It's almost like a vacation. Time to clean out closets, cook something special, or read a book," Janet, the other neighbor, said.

Of course, that wasn't the case with the refugees in the cardboard and tin shacks on the hillsides, or the people who lived on the sampans in various places in the harbor.

The rain began with much cheering. Finally, a normal typhoon with heavy rains had come our way. The reservoirs would begin to fill up again, and we would be over the severe water rationing.

We went to bed on Thursday night hearing the noise of wind and rain outside, but knowing safety inside those twelve-inch-thick brick walls. However, by morning, we had a flood in the living room. The solid rail and a clogged drain on the veranda made the mess. It made a good story to tell—living on the third floor and having eight inches of water in the living room. It drained out in a few hours after I crawled out the window and cleaned the drain on the veranda.

Martha, our social-worker housemate, volunteered as a hostess at the US Servicemen's Center on the Hong Kong side. A chaplain was in charge of the center in the South China Fleet Club building right across the street from Fenwick Pier. All American servicemen who came in on R and R had to come ashore at that pier.

Martha helped plan activities for the center. A hike up Victoria Peak was on the schedule for a Saturday in June, and she asked Bobbie Jo and me to go with her. I wanted to keep busy, so that I wouldn't worry so much. So I agreed and met the group at the time and place she said.

The plan was to walk to the Peak Tram and follow the footpath (at times a 45 percent angle) beside it to the top. That way if anyone couldn't make it all the way up, they could catch the tram and meet the group at the top.

The chaplain explained this plan again about halfway up the steep incline as we rested at a tram stop.

"Why are you looking at me when you say that?" I asked.

"Because your face is so red," he said. He was a single man in his late thirties, good-looking, with dark hair and blue eyes. Martha said he was a Lutheran from Iowa.

"I'm okay," I said. "It's just that my legs are shorter and can't take such long steps, so I have to walk farther to keep up." But I made it to the peak, and we all rode down on the tram.

I could see that Martha was interested in him personally, not just as the center chaplain. I thought about how I felt at times about Bryan. Would he turn up unexpectedly again sometime?

Another Saturday I went with Martha to take the fellows swimming at Shek O, out on the far south reaches of the lacy Hong Kong shoreline. The chaplain drove the big old Terraplane car with a left-hand drive that the center had inherited. The servicemen seemed so young; most of them were just out of high school before going into the service, and now had already had a tour in Vietnam. I talked to one fellow who was from Missouri. He made me think of Jon when we were that age. I told him about Jon, and he was sympathetic, patting me on the shoulder.

I thought about how Jon liked swimming. I'm an okay swimmer, but never loved it like Jon did. One time, when Jon and his friends were horsing around, his best friend hit his head on the side of the pool and went to the bottom. No one noticed, but I saw it from where I lay sunning.

"Jon, Jon, Bob is hurt," I called.

Jon looked, then jumped in and pulled Bob to the side of the pool. By that time, the lifeguard and the other friends were there to help. Jon turned Bob on his stomach and cleared his mouth, then began pushing on his back. It took only a few minutes to start Bob breathing, and then coughing, he sat up. He held his head in his hands, and we took him to the hospital. They kept him overnight, but he was fine.

After that Jon would never horse around while swimming. If others started to, Jon would just walk away.

After swimming for a while that day at Shek O, the group set out to walk around the half-circle beach to a headland across the small bay.

"I'll stay here and sun," I said. But really I wanted to think about Jon and pray a bit. *Isn't there something else I could be doing? It's so hard just to sit and wait after the excitement in Vietnam.*

I must have fallen asleep, because the sun had set when the group got back. They teased me about my red face again, but this was from the sun. I looked around for the guy I had talked with but couldn't see him.

"Where's Joe?" I asked.

"Oh, he decided to swim back across the bay. But he should be back by now," the chaplain said.

We all began to look, but no Joe. The darkness was closing in fast now.

"I'll get the lifeguards. They've already left their tower," the chaplain said.

In a moment, he was back. "They want $50.00 to get the rescue boat out, since they will be working overtime. You girls have any money to help the collection?"

He knew the young guys had little or no money, or they probably wouldn't be on a center activity.

Together, we found enough money. The lifeguards pulled out the long green boat with outriggers and set out rowing across the bay. They were back in about fifteen minutes, with Joe clinging to an outrigger.

They came up on the beach, and I could hear Joe breathing hard. "Thanks. Thanks. I was tired before I was even halfway across," he said.

It was a subdued group that piled into the big old car and rode back to the pier.

Weeks had slipped by, and still no word about Jon. Had my trip been worthless? I wondered about Thai and Minh. Would they recover okay? I called George Bradley, and he promised to call me the minute he had any news.

One afternoon, a loud banging of pots and pans came from the kitchen. The young cook and the older washerwoman were arguing. Martha walked past my conversation teacher and me to the kitchen, but came right back.

"Miss AuYeung, would you help us? I can't understand what they are saying."

"Yes, I'll try," she answered. "Ask them to come here."

Martha returned to the kitchen, and in a few moments, came with the two servants to the dining room. All sat down, and Miss AuYeung talked to them for a few minutes.

"It seems that A` Oi, your cook, is pregnant. A` Saam, your washerwoman, says it is not proper for A` Oi to use the same tub to wash her clothes that A` Saam uses. That is the Chinese custom. A` Oi just found out that she was pregnant because her periods are irregular. You need to buy another tub, so each can use her own. A` Oi says the baby is due in about four or five months."

The two went back to the kitchen satisfied, and we had a very good meal that night.

I wondered what Jon was eating that night. Had he been found? Or was he still in a bamboo cage in the jungle like the picture I had seen in the newspaper that morning? And where was Bryan/Rob, who said he wanted to help get Jon out since "they needed Jon"? Would I ever see him again?

Chapter Nine

The summer advanced with a couple more typhoon approaches, and I was still in the dark about Jon. At home, my parents would be harvesting the garden, freezing, and canning. The papers said the conflict in Vietnam was heating up. That would make it more difficult to rescue Jon.

Our first-year language study was finished, and we had a couple of weeks off. Our neighbor, Janet, had asked me to go with her to Taiwan along with some Chinese ladies. But when the shipping company heard we were foreigners, they refused to let us accompany the Chinese ladies. Foreigners were not allowed to travel deck passage. So we looked for another vacation trip that I could afford after that expensive visit to the States. Something had been said about reimbursing me for the trip, but I hadn't paid much attention. I didn't mind raiding my savings account if it meant rescuing Jon.

"Connie, look here at this freighter trip." Janet hurried into our living room through the door cut in the wall dividing our veranda from theirs, carrying a newspaper. "It is ten days long, here to Bangkok and back, on a Norwegian freighter, and pretty cheap." Her gray-streaked blond hair bobbing, she smiled at me. Janet loved to travel on her time off, but was always short of money, so looked out for the low-priced trips. I think she considered me a partner in economy adventure.

George Bradley, at the consulate, wished me a restful time when I told him of our plans and promised to forward any message about Jon.

An elderly couple and we two were the only passengers on the freighter. Our cabins faced the open deck, and the louvered inner doors allowed the ocean breezes to cool them.

The officers of the ship were Norwegian, although they spoke English well. The crew was all Chinese. The officers didn't like for us to talk to the crew in Chinese; they themselves spoke in pidgin English to the crew. It was Janet talking in Chinese. My Cantonese was still mostly in my mind, not much yet on my tongue.

Lunch was the main meal of the day, with the tubby captain in a fresh white uniform shirt and shorts at the head of the round table. Breakfast and supper were "serve ourselves" with the first officer or engineer eating with us at night.

On the second day, the captain told us that we were passing by Vietnam, but far off the coast. I could see only water, but I stood at the rail for a long time thinking about Jon, where he was and under what conditions. My time there had no reality, although the handle of my suitcase still bore the scars of the bullet's penetration and the threat to my own life.

The ship arrived in Thai waters on Saturday morning, but the twenty-five-mile trip up the river and docking took several hours. Frances Moore, a friend of Janet's, another missionary, met the ship and drove us to her house. She had a friendly, open face, a slight build, and about as much gray in her brown hair as Janet had. They had gone to college together during World War II.

"Take off your shoes inside," Frances told us as we got out of the car. She was in her late forties, but her body was as firm and agile as a younger woman's. "The house has dark wood floors, and dust shows easily."

Jim and Jeanne Hill, other friends of Janet's, called to invite us to lunch with them on Sunday at the Arawan Hotel. "They have a Sunday buffet that is spectacular, and not really expensive," Jeanne said.

So after going to church with Frances and not understanding a word of the Thai spoken, we went on to the Arawan.

"This is the nicest hotel in Bangkok, I think," Frances said as she parked the car and we walked through the spacious lobby to the elevator. A group of local people, the women dressed in elegant jewel-toned Thai silks and the men in dark suits, also waited for the lift. Taller than any of them was an American man, striking in a dark blue silk suit.

Rob, I thought. *It had to be Bryan/Rob.* What was he doing in Bangkok?

He turned to say something to the Thai woman by his side, and in turning, looked straight at me. I saw him start and the recognition in his eyes. Then he looked down at the woman and continued talking.

The group filled the elevator, and we waited for another. I was in a daze. Rob looked tanned and rested. No uniform or casual jacket and trousers like he had worn in Hong Kong. *He was being very attentive to the Thai woman,* I thought. I had once thought I knew him and maybe cared about him and that he returned the caring, but today he hadn't even spoken to me.

We were shown to a table where I had to look directly at the place where the other group was seated. I watched as Rob was positioned and served as the guest of honor.

It was puzzling. Was he on some sort of special mission?

"Connie? Connie?" Janet was talking to me, and I hadn't heard a thing that was said.

"Yes, Janet?"

"Are you going to the buffet and get some food, or just sit here all day?"

I got up and followed the others. I'm sure it was a beautiful table and excellent food, but I remember none of it. My mind was on Rob.

The Hills showed Janet and me around Bangkok that afternoon. Jim was middle-aged, a tall, thin man, with a neat mustache. Jeanne was equally tall, but about twice the size of Jim, with a face still pretty. We were a snug fit in the "Beetle" car they drove.

"This is the SEATO building. It's built on a floating foundation," Jim said.

"What does that mean?" Janet asked. "Does it float on water? Or what?"

"It's in the way it was built. I don't know how," Jim said.

"Does it float on air?" Janet pursued the idea.

"Janet, I have told you all I know. There is no need to keep asking. I don't know anymore." Jim laughed.

"Thai people are relaxed about life. They say, 'There's fish in the *klongs* and rice in the fields, why should I worry?'" Jeanne said. We passed over one of the many canals or *klongs* as Jeanne talked. "Outside of Bangkok are fields of rice almost as large as the wheat fields in Kansas. There is rice to export, as well as to feed their own people."

"Frances is taking you to see the floating market on the river and the *Wat Arun*, the Temple of the Dawn, tomorrow," Jim said. "We'll go to the *Wat Pho* to see the gigantic, reclining, gold-leafed Buddha this afternoon."

Later, back at Frances's house, we found a message for me. Someone at the American Embassy had asked that I come to the embassy the next morning at nine.

Frances had an appointment, so couldn't take me. Next morning, she walked with me to a main street, put me in a cab, and explained to the driver where to take me.

"Have someone at the embassy put you back in a cab, and here is my address in Thai. Do you enough *bapt* to pay the taxi there and back?" She looked at the wad of Thai money I had and sorted out some bills. "Yes, you'll need this much going, and the same coming back."

Traffic in Bangkok was as bad as in Hong Kong in the early morning. Frances thought we had allowed enough time, but I was about fifteen minutes late in getting to the embassy. As I was trying to explain to the receptionist that I didn't know who wanted to see me, someone took my elbow and hustled me across the floor.

"I'll take her to her appointment," he said.

"Rob, what's going on?"

"Wait a minute."

We walked to an elevator, then up to the third floor, and down the hall to an office marked "Storage Room." All the time, he was still holding my arm, but saying nothing. Inside, he pulled out a straight chair for me and another for himself. Most of the room was filled with wooden crates.

"What are you doing in Bangkok?" His tone betrayed his impatience with me. "You could still ruin our plan."

"And what is your plan?" I asked.

"We now know where Jon is, but haven't been able to get a search-and-rescue team in close enough to free him without a lot of casualties. We've had a few other fires to put out that have kept us busy. I'm here now to try to get help from some Thai groups. Yesterday you were with some well-known missionaries. That's not the sort of people my Thai group associates with. But I almost blurted out your name when I saw you."

We talked for a few minutes. I told him that I was on a brief vacation from language study, and how could I know that I would run into him? Then Rob said he had to go.

"I'll have an embassy car take you back to your friend's. I don't want you seen coming out of the embassy and taking a cab right now."

We went down to the ground floor and out the back door to the car park. Rob showed the address to the driver. I got in the backseat, and Rob shut the door.

Who was Rob anyway? He seemed to negotiate with some odd groups, maybe even criminal groups. Could they help him rescue Jon? All these months, Jon had been a captive. Was he in a bamboo cage in the jungle?

As the car pulled out of the embassy parking lot, past the front of the building, I saw Rob getting in a taxi with a Thai woman. So that's the reason he didn't want me to leave by the front door. Perhaps it was the woman he seemed attentive to yesterday. Maybe she had something to do with the group that might help rescue Jon.

Chapter Ten

We sailed on the freighter Tuesday morning for a smooth three-day return to Hong Kong. When I got back to Frances's house on Monday, the time had passed for going to the floating market. So that will have to wait for another trip. We did go on the river and happened to see the royal barges, then to the *Wat Arun* and looked around that temple, decorated with the pieces of broken pottery from a shipwreck. Then we boarded the freighter Monday night for an early departure the next morning.

Back at 169 Boundary, I felt ready to begin again studying Cantonese. In a way, it seemed odd that I needed to be able to speak Cantonese in order to teach English at a refugee college. But I was beginning to understand that in order to live meaningfully in Hong Kong, I needed to be able to speak Cantonese. I intended to live in Hong Kong for several years. True, there were British and some Americans that had lived here for a long time and didn't speak the language, but they basically lived on the surface of life, separated from the people by a wide gulf.

I heard nothing more about Jon. I talked to George Bradley, and he had no news. Would Jon ever be freed? Was he in some cage where he couldn't stand erect? What would he be like when he was rescued after such a long time of confinement? I felt depressed and discouraged by the news that I read in the *Tiger Standard*. One of the neighbors had a shortwave radio and could pick up BBC news. What she relayed to me was that the conflict was heating up in Vietnam and the guerillas always targeted the American advisors. Several had been killed, particularly those who had been featured in an article in a newsmagazine.

I was allowed to begin teaching part-time at this point, an exciting prospect. It had been difficult to adjust to being a student again, and now I could have some ego relief by teaching one course, English 101, to English majors at the college.

The college met in a building borrowed from a boys' school (kindergarten through high school). The principal of the high school was also the acting president of the college. The government called these refugee colleges postsecondary schools. They could not grant degrees, only offer diplomas, which were recognized by several American universities. Since they were organized on the four-year American plan, the government had a hard time reconciling them with their British three-year model.

The first day of classes, I asked my class to write essays telling me about themselves. After several questions, they settled down to writing, and I got interesting papers. One told about being the child of a second wife and complained about the children of the first wife getting all the benefits and how unfair it was. This arrangement of men having two families at the same time and the families knowing about each other was hard for me to understand.

One student was from Saigon. He was ethnically Chinese, although the family had lived in Vietnam for many years. His family owned a brass factory in the countryside and several stalls in the city where the brass was sold, and the young man worked in the stalls often. I wondered why he was telling me so much detail about the making and selling of brass. It had to be a coincidence that I had bought brass in Saigon in the spring. He wouldn't remember me, even if he saw me. There were other American women in Vietnam.

But I worried. Could something still come out that would make Jon suffer more?

After the next class meeting, several students waited to speak to me. The last one walked with me out of the room to the open passageway that ran along the outside of the classrooms.

"Did you like the brass you bought in Saigon?" he asked.

"Why do you think I bought brass in Saigon?"

125

"Because I sold the candle holders to you. You spoke a few words in Cantonese, then started talking in English. My family speaks Cantonese, so I immediately noticed you. I didn't recognize you at first since your hair is longer now." He smiled as he spoke. I could tell he felt proud of himself for remembering me.

Oh, my. I had been right to worry.

"Sorry;, I have to see someone here," I said as I ducked into the dean's office.

As soon as I got back to 169 Boundary, I phoned George Bradley at the consulate.

"Is it going to ruin chances for Jon?"

"I don't know. It has been some time since you went to that meeting for Jon. Surely it won't hurt. But I will ask someone more directly involved."

It was a couple of days before he called back. The consensus was that no harm was done, but everyone was glad to be told about the possible leak that I had been in Saigon at that particular time. Hopefully it would not be talked about, so that the word wouldn't spread.

The very next night, I got a call from Bryan/Rob.

"We've got Jon." He talked fast, and lots of noise on the line made it difficult to understand him.

"Would you repeat that?" I asked.

"We've rescued Jon. But he is in a bad way. His treatment hasn't been good in these last few days. He's being sent to the army hospital at Camp Kue, Okinawa. Will you go to see him?"

"Yes, of course, I'll go to see him. When will he arrive in Okinawa?"

"Tomorrow morning, I think. Maybe you'd better wait until Saturday morning to go. Now, expect that he will look bad when you see him."

I went to call my parents immediately. I decided to go to the cable and wireless office in the Peninsula Hotel, where I could get a clearer connection. The call was put through in a few minutes. I had a hard time remembering that the switch on the radiophone was still done by hand, and I must wait a second in order for the others to hear all of what I had to say.

"Mom, Dad, Jon has been rescued. He will be in the hospital on Okinawa for a while. I'll go up to see him on Saturday."

"Oh, Connie, I'm so relieved to know that he is safe now. Do you need any money for the trip?" my dad asked.

"Connie, do you know any details?" My mother was on the extension phone. I could hear her crying.

"No, only that his condition is not too good. I don't know how he was rescued. I hope there were no casualties in the operation."

Our three minutes ran out before they finished asking questions. My dad would put some money in my account at the bank.

I made arrangements to be gone over the weekend. Martha would teach my Bible study class at the Mandarin-language church. I planned to come back on Sunday night.

Only a couple of flights to Tokyo stopped in Naha. I was on the earliest one on Saturday, and an hour and a half later, I was in Naha. This time no one met me. I was on my own.

I found a Travelers' Aid desk and asked about how to get to Camp Kue and the hospital.

"You will have to take a taxi," an American woman with dark hair and blue eyes at the desk said. "Taxis are not expensive. We use American money here, so you don't have to change money. Are you visiting someone in the hospital? Will you need a place to stay tonight?" The blue eyes were kind, but she gave no time between questions to answer.

"Yes, I am visiting my brother in Camp Kue hospital. Yes, I will need a place to spend the night. Is there a hotel near the hospital?"

"The chaplains at the several bases and camps maintain a guest room for off-island family visiting someone in the hospital. I'll make arrangements for you if you'll tell me your name."

She phoned and was able to reserve a guest room for me, then wrote out the instructions on how to get there.

The taxi took about thirty minutes to get to the hospital; the speed limit was twenty-five miles an hour all over the island.

Naha was a gray city. The Japanese-style houses were unpainted, so had weathered to gray. The businesses were in new, cement-colored square buildings, with only an occasional spot of color from a bright advertising signboard.

Once out of Naha, the highway ran along the waterfront. The clear sky and warm sun made the water blue and sparkling. I could see a freighter passing on the horizon. I felt a stranger and very much alone.

The taxi turned into the drive of a tall, probably ten stories, white, modern building and stopped.

"Hospital, Camp Kue," the driver said.

I got out, paid the driver, and walked into the wide lobby. On the far side was the information desk, with several "pink ladies" waiting to help me.

"I'd like to see Jon Osborne, please."

The lady looked in the file. "I don't find that name. Has he just come in?"

"He was to come in yesterday from Vietnam."

"Oh, then he would be on the seventh floor. They have a separate file at the nurses' station on that floor. You can take the elevator at the back of the lobby up to seven."

I found the elevator and went to the seventh floor. The nurses' station was just beyond the elevator lobby.

"I'd like to see Jon Osborne," I said.

"He just came in yesterday evening. I don't know if he's allowed visitors yet or not. I'll go see." The nurse walked off to the right.

"The doctor is still with him," the nurse told me when she returned. "In about fifteen minutes, you can see him for a few minutes. His condition is not stable."

I sat in a waiting area at the end of the hall until the nurse called me. Then I walked slowly into the room. I was scared of what I would find. If he was treated badly, what had they done to hurt Jon? Was he conscious? Would he know me?

I tiptoed to the bed, the only one in the small room. I saw a figure in the bed, with blond hair showing above the bandages and lots of tubes and wires connected to overhead stands. One brown eye looked at me, and his swollen lips moved. The other eye was shut. The face was so battered and bruised that I wouldn't have recognized Jon. He looked like he had been hit many times in the face and shoulders with a two-by-four.

Brown eyes? Jon didn't have brown eyes. One of our differences was that while I had brown eyes like our father, Jon had our mother's blue eyes. Who was this?

Chapter Eleven

I looked at the nurse standing by. What could I say? And to whom could I say it? Was it another subterfuge, such as I had participated in? Or didn't Rob know that this wasn't Jon?

I looked at the patient. He seemed to be conscious and trying to say something. I leaned closer to his misshapen mouth.

I couldn't understand for sure, but thought he said, "Jon's okay."

I raised my head, looked at him, and began to talk. I told him about calling our parents, about my English class in Hong Kong, and on and on. I looked around and saw that the nurse had slipped out and we were alone.

I leaned close. "Is Jon okay? Is that what you said? Maybe you could blink once if you want to say yes."

The good brown eye blinked once.

"You want me to not say anything?" Again the eye blinked once.

"Okay, for now, you are Jon."

The eye seemed to relax and soon closed in sleep.

I stayed with him until the nurse told me time was up.

"You can visit him again this evening for a few minutes," the nurse said.

I went out into a waiting room, not knowing what to do or say. I sat down and thought for a while. I felt I ought to let someone know that the patient wasn't Jon. But he relaxed and slept only after I promised to keep quiet. I got up and walked to the end of the corridor, then back. Where was Jon? Was he still in the cage in the jungle? Or had all the prisoners in that camp been rescued? If so, where were they? I knew this was something I wouldn't read about in the papers.

I flopped down on a couch. I felt puzzled and helpless. I had no one here that I could talk to. Perhaps I should go to the guest room and rest for a while if it wasn't too far away. I went to the nurses' desk and asked about the location of the guest room. They referred me to the chaplain's office there in the hospital.

Down on the main floor, I found the chaplain's office. A private sat at a desk reading a copy of the *Stars and Stripes*.

"The chaplain on duty is at his office at the chapel. I'll phone him about the guest room," the young private said.

In a moment, he turned and handed the phone to me. "The chaplain would like to talk to you," he said.

The chaplain offered to have a car pick me up and take me to the guest quarters. He asked if I would like to talk to a chaplain.

"Yes," I said, "that would be good."

I waited there in the office until the chaplain himself walked in. He was an older man, not tall but still trim, with gray hair and kind eyes.

"Miss Osborne, I think you said that you have visited your brother. How did you find him?"

"He's been beaten pretty badly. His face looks like a mashed potato. Only his hair and one eye are showing."

"Well, I'll drive you over to the guest quarters, and we can talk on the way."

We drove along the oceanfront for a few miles until we came to a fenced area. "Kadena Air Force Base," the sign over the gate said.

"The guest quarters that we have for hospital visitors are here at Kadena. Did you fly in from the States today?" the chaplain asked.

"No, I live in Hong Kong. I'm an English teacher for a college there. Or will be. I'm still learning Cantonese, so only teach one course now. So when they called that Jon was here, I came right up."

"How was Jon hurt?" he asked.

"He's been in a cage in the jungle in Vietnam after being kidnapped by the communist guerillas. He wasn't mistreated until recently, I hear."

It all came flowing out. I felt that this was a person I could talk freely with and he would not betray my confidence. It was so good to be open about my concerns. But I didn't tell him that the patient wasn't Jon.

"Would you like for me to pray with you for Jon now?" the chaplain asked.

"Oh, yes, please do."

After the prayer that reminded me that we were in the care of the Lord, I followed him into the barracks-style wooden building. My room on the second floor was clean and neat, but khaki plain. *Well, that's okay,* I thought. *I just want a safe, clean place to rest.*

I slept for about an hour and awoke suddenly, not knowing where I was. I heard the noise of an airplane landing nearby. Then another, and still another. *I must be near the flight line, and no one here sleeps in the late afternoon.* I straightened my clothes, combed my hair, and went downstairs. Another private sat at a desk with a phone.

"Could you call a taxi for me to go to the hospital at Camp Kue?"

"Sure," he said and picked up the phone.

Back at the hospital, I went first to the nurses' station on the seventh floor.

"May I see Jon Osborne now?"

"You're his sister?" A different nurse was on duty.

"Yes, I am. How is he?"

"He slept some, and his condition is more stable," the nurse said.

She walked with me to Jon's room, and we found him awake. The swelling had gone down some, and the shape of his face below the bandages was beginning to show.

I pulled up a chair and sat down on the side of the bed, where he could see me with his one good eye. I began to talk again. I talked about our parents and home. Perhaps he would need to know this information. I felt that I was blundering around in the dark. How could I help the situation when I didn't know what the situation was?

The door opened, and two men came in. One in a white coat came up to the bed and began examining Jon, so I assumed he was a doctor. I turned around and saw that the other man in uniform was standing at the window with his back turned to me. But I knew that back.

"Rob?" I said as I walked over to him.

He turned a tired, lined face to me. Had he been part of the rescue attempt and not slept since?

He put an arm around me.

"When we saw the bright hair, we were sure that we had Jon. We tried to get a message in to him. Maybe the guerillas found out and moved Jon. Or maybe Jon thought it best not to be rescued. Of course, we opened all the cages, but we thought he was the only American, that all the others were Vietnamese and that they would be able to find their own way to safety. If Jon was there, he must have hidden somehow. Covered his head, and he didn't speak. The helicopter couldn't take them all." His voice broke. "I'm sorry that I jumped at the chance to call you before I could talk to him."

I tried to swallow the lump in my throat and leaned my head on his shoulder. They may have left Jon to find his own way to safety in the Vietnamese jungle!

"You need some rest," I said. "Have you had anything to eat since you went on the rescue mission?"

He shook his head.

"Come on; he doesn't need us with the doctor here. I haven't eaten today either. We'll go down to the cafeteria and get some food."

We got plates of rice with beef and tomatoes. Rob was almost asleep in his chair.

"Where will you stay tonight?" I asked. "I have a room at the chaplains' guesthouse on Kadena."

"I can stay at the BOQ, I guess."

We took a taxi first to the Kadena BOQ, then the taxi took me on to the guesthouse. I had never seen Rob when he wasn't in control of the situation, when he needed help. Always before I was the one who needed help or asked the wrong questions or turned up at the wrong places.

I went to the 9:00 a.m. service at the chapel, then got a taxi to the hospital. My plane left for Hong Kong at 3:00 p.m., so my visit with Jon would be short.

The sun was clear and bright, making the day warm. The humidity was beginning to drop here, as it did in Hong Kong in the fall. The grass was still green, and the poinsettias were five feet tall along the chapel wall, with their top leaves just beginning to turn red.

But when I got to the seventh floor, I found a "No Visitors" sign on the door of Jon's room. I went to the nurses' desk and asked about him.

"He's come down with a virus of some kind. Probably something he picked up in the jungle. His wounds seem to be healing. But the virus will set him back some. We don't know what kind of virus it is, so we feel it would be unwise to allow any visitors."

"So I can't see him at all today? I'm going back to Hong Kong this afternoon, so this is my last chance to see him." I felt relieved in a way, because I didn't know what to talk about to him, yet I wanted to see him and tell him I wished him well, but that I needed to go back to Hong Kong.

Rob got out of the elevator as I stood talking to the nurse. I listened as the nurse told him the same story.

"Are you going back to Hong Kong today?" Rob asked me.

"Yes, my plane leaves at three. That's the only plane on Sunday. I didn't make any arrangements for my class at the college on Monday. So I need to get back. But does he really have a virus, or is this just so I can't see him?"

"I see you have your bag with you. Do you want to get some lunch, then I'll go with you to the airport?" He ignored my question.

"First I want to write a note to say I tried to see him and tell him good-bye." I looked around, then dug a pen out of my purse as the nurse handed me some notepaper.

I gave the folded note to the nurse, and Rob and I went down the elevator.

"A fellow at the BOQ told me about a nice restaurant not too far away. Is that okay for lunch?"

"Sure," I said.

We didn't talk much while we ate in a Japanese-style steak house, each busy with our own thoughts. Jon must have kept quiet when the cages were being opened. If he had said a word, they would have known he was an American. Was he not able to say anything? Jon was usually actively participating in anything going on. Maybe he knew this guy needed to go to a hospital right then. And he thought he could handle himself in the jungle. That would be like Jon. What was I going to say to our parents? This would be a hard blow.

In the taxi going to Naha to the airport, we were still quiet. But in the waiting room after I had checked in, Rob began to talk. He took one of my hands in his.

"I have to say, we no longer know where Jon is. I can only hope that if he escaped, that he will soon find help, because he will have only limited strength. He does speak Vietnamese well, and with some help to cover or color his hair, he might pass for a peasant."

"How could you leave him in the jungle?" I asked. "I'm sorry; I know that you did the best you could." I sighed, picturing Jon alone in the jungle. I remember him at nine or ten years old and he loved adventure in the woods, but would he feel that way now? He probably already had his fill of it.

I continued, "I know that he has a strong faith to help him. Yesterday, when the chaplain took me to the guesthouse, he prayed, asking God's care for all involved. He didn't know that he was praying for two Jons that both need His mercy and care, but God knows. By the way, I don't like this hearing from you just now and then. You could write me a note occasionally and tell me what is happening. And what do I say to my parents? Is it okay to tell them that this isn't our Jon?"

"They know about your trip to Vietnam in the spring?"

"Yes, they know I went, but not all the details."

"Go ahead and tell them, but ask them to keep it quiet, if they can," he said.

We sat holding hands until the flight was called. Rob hugged me to him and surprised me by kissing me hard. Then I trudged out to the plane. I felt discouraged, caught in a web of unknowns. What could I do when the search-and-rescue team had tried and failed? How could I help Jon? I wished that I could go back to Vietnam and look for Jon myself. At least I would know him on sight.

Chapter Twelve

Back in Hong Kong, I took a taxi home to 169 Boundary. As soon as I dropped off my bag, I left to go to the cable and wireless office. I had to call my parents, and I didn't want a bad connection.

"Mom, is Dad on the line, too? I need to talk to both of you."

I told them about the mix-up and how no one knew where Jon was now, but all hoped that he was free and working his way to safety. I had ordered six minutes this time, but they were still asking questions and trying to comfort me when the time was up.

Martha and Bobbie Jo had a lot of questions later that evening. For the first time, I answered their questions, although I didn't volunteer any information. They could tell how discouraged I was, and the three of us prayed together for Jon.

That night I dreamed that Jon was still held in the jungle by the guerillas and was being beaten to a pulp. I was watching but could do nothing, being entangled in that same jungle. I woke up sweating and crying. I asked God if there wasn't something I could do to help Jon.

On Monday, I had my language classes, then went to the college to teach my English class. The student from Saigon met me in the outside passageway and spoke again in his friendly way.

"I'm sorry I couldn't talk with you the other day," I said. "I did buy some brass in Saigon in the spring, but I went off on my own and the people here don't know about it. My twin brother was kidnapped by the guerillas and is being held in the jungle. I hoped to find out something in Saigon about him."

I was talking too much to a student, telling him more than I had anyone. I had better shut up.

"Tell me your name. I haven't learned all the names in class yet."

"My name is Yeung Yau Kwong. My friends call me Kwong."

Class started, and I pushed Vietnam to the back of my mind.

A few days later, I saw Kwong on the street leading to the college. I had caught a bus across Prince Edward Road from 169 Boundary and was walking from the bus stop on Waterloo Road through the high school grounds to the college.

"Teacher, a relative, Yeung Yau Thai, has come from Vietnam for some special surgery at a hospital here in Hong Kong. Perhaps you met him when you were in Saigon?"

Thai? Did he mean Thai that was wounded in the guerilla attack on the way to Dalat airport?

"I did meet a man named Thai in Saigon. He was wounded in an attack by guerillas. Is it the same one?"

"I think so. I visited him last night and told him about you being my teacher. Would you visit him in Queen Mary Hospital?" Kwong asked.

"Perhaps I could this evening. When are visiting hours?"

"Until nine. I'm going again; I could show you the way," Kwong offered.

We worked out when and where to meet at the Star Ferry to go over to the Hong Kong side, then walked on together to the college.

That evening we arrived at the hospital ward to find it filled with ten beds, five on each long wall. Lights and fans on long tubes came down from the high ceiling to cool the room. The antiseptic smell common to hospitals assaulted my nose. Kwong headed for the third bed on the right, but saw that the white curtains were drawn about the bed.

A nurse in a blue uniform and a white coif was coming toward us and spoke as we stopped. "This patient had surgery this afternoon, so is sedated. Perhaps you could come back tomorrow."

"I'm sorry, Teacher. He thought his surgery wouldn't be for another day."

We left, making plans to try again.

Two nights later, I had a phone call from Thai. His voice wasn't as strong as it had been in Vietnam.

"Miss Osborne, this is Thai. I'm sorry I couldn't speak to you when you came with my cousin to visit. I got your phone number from him."

"Thai, how are you? I'm sorry that your recovery has been so long. I had hoped that you would be well long before this."

"This was only a small reconstruction surgery, to help my shoulder work better. I'm really very well. Have you heard anything about Jon?"

"Thai, do you know that Rob thought they had rescued Jon? But when I went to the army hospital on Okinawa, the man they rescued wasn't Jon." I was sad to have to tell Thai the bad news.

"Have you heard from Rob?"

"Yes, he was on Okinawa, and I saw him."

I told Thai about the mix-up and the theories about Jon's present location.

"Miss Osborne, let me think about this. Would you come to see me here at the hospital tomorrow?"

I agreed to come in the evening after all my classes were finished.

At the hospital, I found the curtains open away from the bed, and Thai sitting in a chair. He got up and came toward me, smiling.

"Perhaps we could walk out on the terrace and talk," he said.

Once on the terrace, we found some chairs and sat down. Queen Mary Hospital is mid-level up the Peak. The sun was setting out over where the mouth of the river that goes up to Canton joins the China Sea. Junks, patrol boats, and even sampans were hurrying here and there on the water. The sky glowed orange, then softened into magenta and deep pink.

"If Jon was in the group that was released from the cages, then I think I might be able to guess where he would go. Rob is right that he would need help to avoid recapture. If I knew where he was being held, I might figure out where he would head for help. If he was held near Hmong territory, he would head there. Hmongs like Americans, and he would be safe there while he gained his strength."

"I've not heard of the Hmongs. Would they endanger themselves if they help Jon?" I asked.

"Hmongs are a mountain tribal group, not Vietnamese. Jon will be well disguised, and will leave as soon as he is able," Thai said.

"Is there anything I could do that would help get Jon away?"

"I need to think some more. Also, I'll need to talk to Rob. I do not know yet when I will be finished with therapy and be released here. Can you let Rob know that I need to talk to him?"

"I will have to work on that. I don't hear directly from Rob. He just drops in out of the blue, sometimes. Usually when I need him, he appears."

I thought maybe George Bradley at the consulate could help me. I called as soon as I got home to 169 Boundary. He didn't know himself, but would ask about how to contact Rob. "And I'll pass the word that Thai is here in the hospital," he said.

I went to Queen Mary Hospital again the next night to report to Thai that I knew nothing yet. Once again, we went out on the terrace to talk. The pleasant breezes from the ocean brought not-so-pleasant smells from the fish-processing plant down below. We moved to the other side of the terrace, and there found only the fragrant bouquet of the bauhinia, whose orchidlike flowers opened in the cooler fall weather.

Thai was glad of the company but disappointed that I had no news from Rob. As we talked, the door opened, and out came Rob.

"Rob," I cried jumping up. Thai was on his feet also, smiling.

"I got the message that you were here, Thai," he said, as he flung an arm around my shoulders.

I listened to them talk about where Jon had been held and where he might have gone for help in escaping. Finally, I said that I needed to get back across the harbor and got up to leave, since I had class tomorrow.

Rob stood and took my arm. "I'll see you home," he said. Turning to Thai, he said, "I'll come tomorrow morning with some maps, and we'll talk some more."

"That was a quick answer to George Bradley's 'passing the word,'" I said as we got in a taxi at the hospital's entrance.

"Yes, well, I'm always anxious to come to Hong Kong, you know. And worried about Jon."

"Do you think you can find him?" I asked.

"Thai knows more about Jon and about Vietnam than I do. He may not be able to do much, but if he can remember and think, he might have valuable clues to Jon's whereabouts."

On the Kowloon side, Rob put me in a taxi, gave me a peck of a kiss, and said good-bye but not a word about when I would see him again. He was back to being the one in charge, the all-business Rob.

Chapter Thirteen

Thai was released from the hospital and sent back to Saigon to finish his therapy at the Seventh-Day Adventist hospital, where a new American-trained physical therapist worked. He called to tell me his departure time, and I went to the airport to see him off.

"I haven't been able to think about where Jon might be. Rob and I looked over the maps and saw several possibilities. When I get back to Saigon, I'll think, and maybe I'll be able to get some information from Minh and others."

"The Moon Festival is coming up soon. I'll be off school for two days plus the weekend. I'll come to Saigon then," I said.

"I'll count on that," Thai said.

The next day, I got a letter from Bryan/Rob. I was astonished, and I must admit thrilled. It was my first letter from him, and it was almost a love letter. This was from the Bryan I had met first, not the all-business Rob. He said how glad he had been to see me at Queen Mary Hospital, and he hoped that more opportunities to be with me would come soon. I knew, but didn't like, the unspoken fact that in his work, whatever it was, scheduling time off must be difficult. I looked over the envelope, but there was no return address. The postmark was Hong Kong, so he wrote and mailed it while here.

One of our language teachers spent his teaching hour telling us about the Moon Festival and its origin. In a time long ago, the ruler was a cruel tyrant. Rebel factions planned a coup and notified their members by sending moon cakes, with a coded message inside naming the day of the full moon in October as the day of action. So the moon cake has the hard yolk of an egg, or something similar, inside to represent the full moon. I ate a bite of moon cake once, but didn't like the lardy, not sweet, taste.

Now it is a time for lovers to go out to a hilltop and look at the full moon and its reflection in the bay. If a young man didn't ask his girlfriend out during the festival time, she would know that they were breaking up.

I wondered if Bryan/Rob would ask me out during the Moon Festival if he were to be in Hong Kong during that time.

Kwong reported that Thai had arrived in Saigon safely and was enduring the painful therapy. But I heard nothing about Jon's current situation.

On Tuesday before the Moon Festival holidays, I received a cablegram from Thai. He asked me to come to Saigon as soon as possible to help him. So I made arrangements to leave late Wednesday afternoon. I cabled Thai my arrival time, and he sent another relative to meet me at the airport. The relative stood at the arrival gate with a sign saying, "Oborn," but agreed that it was me he was looking for.

"Come, we hurry. Thai waits," he said.

I had brought only my carry-on bag, so we were able to go directly to the car.

It was already dark as we drove, but the wide streets were noisy, still full of cars, motor scooters, and bicycles, even a horse and cart. Girls with their split-skirted *ao dais* flying in the breeze rode sidesaddle behind the drivers of motor scooters.

We met Thai at a restaurant, small and dimly lit. He looked well and strong, but his shoulder seemed stiff as he stood by a round table to greet me.

"Miss Osborne, I'm glad you could come. I have news about Jon's location," he said.

"Oh, I'm so glad. And please, call me Connie."

"Yes, I will call you Connie. Come, sit down, and let's talk."

Jon was in the mountains of the Central Highlands, with the Hmong people that he and Thai had visited before. Thai thought we should fly to an old airfield left from when the French ruled Vietnam near the mountains, then borrow a jeep to drive the rest of the distance. I would have to drive since his shoulder was still stiff; also, I could be sure to get the identification right this time. He had made plane reservations for early the next morning.

Thai and his relative took me to that same hotel that I had stayed in before for the night.

We left at six thirty the next morning, and in an hour and a half were landing at the old airfield, now used only by small planes.

Thai had asked a friend to find a jeep we could use on the mountain roads. The friend, an older man, dressed in black cotton pants and shirt, maybe a veteran of the war for independence from the French, was at the airfield and led us outside to a World War II French jeep. The canvas top was torn and patched, and the paint was mostly gone from the jeep itself.

The friend said something to Thai and laughed.

"My friend says it runs great even if it looks terrible," Thai said to me. "Here are the keys."

We loaded our small bags and the friend in the back, and I took the keys. Thai rode beside me as I drove to tell me the way. We left the friend in the first village.

Vietnamese celebrate the Moon Festival also, and I saw vendors setting up stands to sell moon cakes on the street in the morning sun. Here it's a harvest festival, too. Fruits and vegetables were piled at storefronts.

The last time I was in Vietnam, guerillas had attacked our car and Thai and Minh had both been shot. I had rolled under the seat into the trunk and avoided harm. I felt nervous about the countryside. Even though the Central Highlands were considered to be safe from the communist guerillas, I could feel the sweat beginning to form on my body.

A light rain cooled the air as we left the village. Small fields near the village had been cleared of trees to grow rice and vegetables, but most were already harvested now.

Once away from the village, the trees came down near the road. This made me more nervous. I worried that communist guerillas could be hiding in the trees ahead, just waiting to attack us. The jeep had no trunk for me to roll into.

"Thai, are you sure that it is safe to drive along this road?"

"Connie, no place in Vietnam is 100 percent safe. But the US Special Forces have been active here, pacifying the Hmong, and during the daylight, it is as safe as it can be."

The road began to rise, and before long the trees thinned.

"It is about one hour's drive to the Hmong village Jon and I visited. I wonder how he was able to travel from where he had been held; he couldn't have walked this far in his condition," Thai said.

The road was becoming rougher and narrower the farther we went.

"Will this road go on to the Hmong village?" I asked. I seemed to be following a trail on the rocks, rather than a real road.

"It does get rougher, but we can get through. Jon and I did last year. You can do it. You drive as well as Jon."

We splashed through shallow streams and bumped over rocks that threatened to overturn the jeep. The air was almost cold in the open vehicle, although the light rain had stopped. It smelled of woods and decaying matter, almost like the woods in Missouri in the fall. I thought of my parents and the disappointment they had suffered when I went to Okinawa and found that it wasn't Jon after all. I hadn't told them about this trip to Vietnam for fear it wouldn't turn out right.

We could see a village up ahead when the engine of the jeep gave a short wheeze and stopped. We rolled to a stop as I tried to restart the engine. I got out, raised the hood, and looked at the insides. I could drive, but I knew nothing about motors. Thai looked and said, "I think my friend was joking when he said it was a good vehicle."

I picked up my small bag and put the strap over my shoulder. "We might as well walk on to the village. There's no one to help out here."

Three quarters of an hour later, we walked into the village. Even though we could see it when the jeep stopped, we had to go down into a valley, then back up before reaching the village. There were two or three stores, but the rest of the ten or twelve small buildings were homes, built close together for protection.

"I'll see if I can find someone who speaks Vietnamese in this Hmong area and ask about any foreigners." Thai walked on ahead.

In a few minutes, Thai called over his shoulder to me. I found him in front of an open doorway, talking with an old man with white hair and a thin, white beard.

"He says that the US Special Forces have moved farther west and north now, but he remembers there was a sick man in the last house in the village; this way." He started walking ahead.

I followed, running a few steps to keep up, past the small wooden houses with thatch roofs and open doors. Thai stopped at the last house and called into the open door.

A voice answered, and they talked back and forth, then a woman came to the door carrying a baby on her back. The baby was so well-wrapped that it appeared that the woman had a humpback. Her bright eyes and smiling face greeted us warmly, although I couldn't understand a word.

"They helped a sick man, not a Hmong or Vietnamese, that her husband found lying on the trail. He spoke Vietnamese well. They thought him to be French, so took him to the Catholic mission near the river. Although they are not Catholics, they think the French missionaries are good people and will help others in trouble, she says," Thai said to me.

Thai thanked the woman and gave her some money.

"The mission is not too far, and it is near the river. That's good," Thai said to me.

After walking almost an hour, Thai and I saw ahead the red tile roof of a building just sticking out over the trees and guessed it to be the mission. I was sweating from the trek across the rough terrain, although it was almost all downhill. I was sure that a blister was forming on my heel. I had dressed in hiking clothes and boots, but I never really expected to walk so far since we had the jeep. I took out my bottle of water and swallowed some as we rested a moment under a kapok tree. I looked out over a lower valley at the mountains in a blue haze across the valley; the nearer mountains were covered in trees and lush foliage. I hadn't noticed that we had come down so much lower as we walked, but the difference showed in the type of trees and bushes, as well as the rise in heat and humidity.

"Quiet," Thai whispered as he pulled me back into the bushes. "Someone is coming. Might be guerillas."

I was hardly breathing when we saw a line of men with rifles traveling along the trail. They were dressed in worn clothes; most had on tan shorts and loose shirts. They wore sandals, some with soles made from old tires. Still, they walked quietly.

We watched them go over the top of the next hill before I breathed easily again.

Then we continued on down the trail toward the group of Western-style brick buildings. One was a church with a cross on the steeple. Next to it was a two-story house. There were several smaller buildings behind these two, and a wall surrounded them all. We paused at the gate of the compound, and Thai said that the sign read "Catholic Mission" in both French and Vietnamese. Thai rang the bell hanging at one side of the gate, and soon a young man came to let us in. He was Vietnamese, but wearing a brown robe, probably a novice at the mission.

Thai talked to the young man, then told me what he said. Yes, they did have a sick man here; and yes, we could see him; just follow him.

He closed the gate behind us, then led us past the church to the two-story house. Inside we climbed the stairs and met a missionary nurse in her white starched uniform in the upper hallway. Thai talked to her in French, I think. She turned and led us to an open door and into a hospital room.

Chapter Fourteen

A man was lying in the only occupied bed of the four in the room, with a mosquito net draped over him. He seemed to be sleeping quietly.

The nurse spoke softly to the man, then lifted the net from around him. He sat up and turned toward us.

"Thai, is that you?" he said in a surprisingly strong voice.

"Jon, Jon, it's good to see you. How are you? And look who is here." Thai hurried to the bedside.

"Connie! How did you get here?"

I hugged his neck, but couldn't say anything for the tears flowing down my face. He felt like a skeleton covered with just skin. His bony arms hugged me, and then he laughed. He wore much-washed pants and a shirt. His blond hair was on his shoulders, and his reddish beard nearly as long.

"Am I dreaming? Will you both just fade away?"

Thai swallowed hard, and then he too laughed. "It's a long story, but we want to know how you got here, and are you able to travel?"

"Sure, I can travel, but not on foot for long. The river is close by, and I was hoping to get a boat down to where I could catch a riverboat to Saigon."

"There's a riverboat? That's great. Can we hire a boat here to take us downriver?" I asked.

"It will be expensive, because of the danger, Connie," Thai said. "I have some money, but not enough."

"I cleaned out my savings account to come. Dad will put more in for me, but what cash I have is limited," I said.

Jon listened to our conversation, then stood up, tottered across the floor to the door, and opened it. "Sister, may we see Father Stephen?" he called to the nurse waiting in the hall.

"I'll send someone to find him and bring him here," she said.

Jon quickly sat down in a chair near the door. Evidently, his strength was minimal. "Tell me how you found me," Jon commanded.

"Thai is the one who worked it out," I said.

Thai rehearsed the events that had led us to continue looking for Jon. I wondered if Bryan knew that we were here searching for Jon. What would he say to me then?

"After I returned to Saigon, I remembered that we had come to this Hmong village last year, so I asked the Special Forces to keep their ears open for any clue that a foreigner might be around here. When I got their report, I cabled Connie to come, and here we are ready to take you back with us."

Father Stephen came. He was in his mid-forties, slightly built, dark hair with some gray, and handsome. He spoke English clearly, but with a French accent. He agreed to advance us some cash in return for my check in US dollars.

"Our young novice comes from a family who has boats. I will ask him to help us find a boat, and go with you to pole the boat through some rapids. I notice that you have a stiff shoulder and couldn't pole much," he said to Thai.

It was late afternoon when the novice returned with the news that he had found a boat we could use.

Father Stephen came to tell us and suggested that we leave as soon as it was dark. "The guerillas often come through here from Laos. The river is narrow here and can be easily crossed. They have left us alone so far, because we will treat their wounded. There are none here now, but more could come at any time. We don't have a real hospital, just this four-bed clinic with the nurses."

We ate a meal with Father Stephen and the nurses. There were small meat rolls to wrap in lettuce leaves, and greens with rice. I was surprised that vegetables could be eaten raw in Vietnam. In Hong Kong, fresh vegetables were still grown with night-soil fertilizer, so they have to be cooked or soaked in bleach. I thought of our meals at home and how much enjoyment we had together as a family. I needed to send word to our parents, but not yet. Wait until we were safely in Saigon, out of danger.

"Your brother has a recurrence of malaria now. That is making him weaker than he was. He will need to rest during this trip," the nurse said to me in French with Thai translating.

Thai and I had our small bags. The nurse gave Jon a smaller bag with colorful embroidery for some medicine to ease the pain and fever. Father Stephen brought still another bag, this one with woven stripes, containing food for our trip.

"God bless and keep you safe," he said as we got in.

The boat was long and narrow, with seats just wide enough for one person to sit. We made a bed for Jon in the bottom of the front end. The novice, Matthew, stood in the rear of the boat and used two long poles to push or sometimes sweep the boat along. The ends that Matthew held crossed just in front of him, and each had a short handle across the pole. I think the other end was similar to a long oar. Farther down, the current would be swift enough to move us along without the poles.

We waved good-bye as Matthew pushed us off with one pole. It was good to be moving in the direction of Saigon with Jon on board.

The boat skirted what seemed to be some shallow ripples. There was no moonlight, so we felt that any guerillas on the heavily wooded bank would not see or take shots at us. Only the sound of the quiet raising and lowering of the poles and the soft hissing of the boat in the water came to my ears.

The monotony made me drowsy. It had been a long, exhausting day since six thirty that morning in Saigon. I had struggled to drive the jeep over rough terrain, had hiked twice, but had found my twin. My head drooped, and my hands loosened their grip on the sides of the boat.

Twang! Something slammed into the top edge of the boat.

"Get down. Get down." Thai was pulling on my leg. Matthew thrust a pole into the edge of the bank and sent us flying out into the middle of the stream.

"The current carried us too close to the edge of the river. I think Matthew was drowsing also, since he didn't have to pole. Someone heard the boat and shot at us," Thai explained.

We surged along in the stronger current, but Matthew watched that we stayed near the center of the water. At this rate, we would arrive at the riverboat dock in plenty of time for its departure the next morning.

I heard Jon muttering something, and then he was thrashing about. Thai and I changed places so I could reach Jon. His face was burning with fever. I found the medicine bag and pulled out the envelopes. Which was the fever medicine? I couldn't see to read the labels, and the envelopes were the same. Thai turned on his pocket flashlight for a moment, and I sorted them out. I put the pill in Jon's mouth and then the flask of water to his lips. After I raised his head, he was able to swallow a bit. I leaned over the side of the boat to wet a cloth and then wiped his face. After a few minutes, he was quieter and slept again.

Back on my seat, I breathed easier, and my heartbeat slowed. Then I heard noise from up ahead. Even in the darkness, I could see a froth of white on the water, and the boat was going faster and faster.

"What is happening?" I spoke just above a whisper to Thai.

"We are coming to the rapids, I think. Father Stephen said that Matthew would steer us through the rapids, remember?"

Mathew said something to Thai, and he relayed it to me. "Hold on." He straddled Jon's form to hold him in the boat.

At that moment, the moon came out from behind a cloud, and we could see the rocks ahead. Matthew used the pole to keep us off the big rocks, and we shot through to the smooth water beyond. I didn't know that I was holding my breath until we were through and I breathed again.

Soon the sky began to show some light. Night was almost over. I didn't know how near we were to the riverboat dock. I prayed we were on time.

Pink and orange shafts shot up into the sky, then the sun came up over the trees on the bank. Full daylight meant dangerous travel as we neared the junction of our smaller tributary with the Mekong, where we would meet the riverboat.

We rounded a big curve in the river and saw ahead the Mekong, and there was the riverboat at its dock. Matthew hugged the shore, where it was shallow enough for him to use his pole, his only way to guide the boat.

We came into the Mekong and surged along in the current that carried us to the far side of the big river, where Matthew could guide us again. I was thankful that Matthew knew this river and how to maneuver into the right current.

We were some time in getting our turn at the small dock where we could step out on the pier. Several bystanders helped to hold the swaying boat and then loaned hands to help get Jon on the pier. I gathered up our bags and said good-bye to the novice. He would get the boat back to the area of the mission by hard work, poling all the way.

Jon was awake, although his mind wasn't clear yet. We moved him to the shade of a small hut beside the pier. Thai went off to see about tickets and when the riverboat sailed.

"Connie, I can't believe that you are here. Why aren't you in Hong Kong?" Jon was perking up. "I'm not as strong as I thought I was."

"Soon we'll be on the riverboat going down to Saigon. Then we'll get you to a hospital, and before long you'll be strong and healthy again." I smiled at the idea of Jon strong and healthy again, as well as free.

I saw Thai coming back.

"I got a cabin with two bunks for you and Jon," he said.

"How about you?" I asked.

"I can travel deck passage, and that'll be fine," he said.

"Your shoulder will really bother you after a night on the deck," I reasoned. "Wasn't there enough money?"

Thai laughed. "I'm accustomed to sleeping on a board with a thin mat on it. That's not much different from sleeping on the deck."

"When does the riverboat sail?" I asked.

"We have about an hour. I can buy some hot noodles from that man over there for our breakfast, if you want," Thai offered.

"Good. I think Father Stephen put fruit in the bag for us."

We boarded the riverboat about half an hour later. It took both Thai and myself to get Jon up, on board, and settled in the room with two bunks. I breathed a sigh of relief. Everything seemed to point that we would get Jon safe to Saigon, then home.

Chapter Fifteen

The riverboat sailed with only a few passengers besides we three. It was a flat-bottomed boat like a barge, with four small cabins on each side behind the high compartment for the helmsman. Large open decks were in front and behind the cabins and bridge. There were cargo crates here and there near the rail.

"Is it usual to have so few passengers?" I asked Thai.

"I talked to one of the crew members. On the way up from Saigon, the guerillas shot at the boat twice. Some bullets hit the boat and injured a passenger. So many are afraid; even some of the crew deserted."

"Will we get through, do you think?" This wasn't good news.

"I think it is the only way we can go. We would need the jeep to go back to the airfield. Jon couldn't walk back. And the small aircraft might get shot at, too."

"You're right. I'll just start praying for safety, and I know Father Stephen is, too.

The riverboat swung out into the main channel of the Dong Nai River and settled down to about five knots. It would take us about a day and a half to get to Saigon.

By the middle of the morning, it was hot on the boat. Even the breeze the motion of the boat made was heating up. The small cabin was soon breathless. An electric fan was mounted on the wall. I turned it to hit Jon on the bottom bunk, opened and fastened back the outer door, and propped the louvered inner door open, too. Then I went out on deck.

A canvas tarp was rigged up to shade part of the deck, and chairs had been set in groups of two or three for passenger use. I sat in one of the chairs and watched the bank slide by. Tall royal palms, shorter flowering trees that I couldn't name, and bushes grew down to the waterline of the river. I saw boys washing their water buffaloes in the shallows near the bank. Once I saw a flock of white geese on the water's edge tended by children. Sometimes villages came right down to the river. One time, a long, narrow, rocky ridge came out from the village to almost the middle of the river. The riverboat blew its horn as we approached and then stopped at the end of the rocky ridge. A man ran out on the ridge and climbed the rope ladder on the side of the boat. Another passenger.

The deck began to smell of hot tar. I walked back to the cabin and found Jon awake and trying to get up.

"Is your fever gone?" I asked as I felt his forehead. "Yes, I guess it is, for the moment, anyway."

He still wore the pants and shirt the nurses had given him. He slipped his feet into the sandals Father Stephen had given him and stood up. He held onto the upper bunk for a moment, then straightened up.

"I'd like to go out on deck. Will you help me?"

"Of course." I took Jon's arm, and we walked slowly down the narrow walkway between the cabin and the deck rail. When we reached the open deck with chairs, Jon sat on the first one.

"I was stronger than this when I was in the cage. I'd forgotten that malaria takes the starch out of me this way."

Thai came up and sat down next to Jon. "How are you feeling this morning?" Thai asked.

"Okay. But still pretty weak. I want you both to tell me about how you came to find me."

"I'll start," I said. "Several months ago, one day in our flat in Hong Kong, someone broke out the windows of my room by shooting marbles with a slingshot from the roof of the building next door. Turns out it was Bryan, who is also known as Rob to Thai."

"Bryan, Rob, who is that?" Jon looked puzzled.

"He said he met you in Saigon. Maybe he used still another name; I have only heard two," I said.

We looked at Thai. He seemed reluctant to say anything, then muttered a word in Vietnamese.

Jon looked surprised, then said, "Oh."

Thai told about the trip I made to the meeting with the village leaders and how he'd been shot. Then I told about seeing Bryan in Bangkok in August and the false start in Okinawa, then talking to both Thai and Bryan in Hong Kong a few weeks ago.

"But tell us how you got free and up to the Hmong territory," Thai said.

"When I was first captured, I was treated quite well. I was in a hut, but free to walk about the hut—and outside with a guard at times. They fed me what they were eating. I kept pretty fit. Then they brought in a couple of Vietnamese local government officials, then later three more, so they were stricter about our movements. We were some distance from Dalat, but I don't know how far.

"Then they moved deeper in the jungle and built the cages deep in the underbrush. That meant that they could leave us almost alone when they went on their raids. When the other American was captured, they had trouble. He didn't speak Vietnamese and rebelled at every command. The guards were so angry that they beat on him all the time. I knew that he would be dead in a short time. When the helicopter landed that night, only two guards had stayed behind to keep us. They were out of commission quickly. Then the Americans started opening the cages, looking at everyone in the face. They saw the blond hair and knew that they had found an American. I pulled a black cloth over my head and didn't speak in English. I knew they couldn't take us all, so I let them take the other guy. He needed medical care immediately.

"I traveled as long as I could. One of the Vietnamese prisoners guided me to his home for food. But we both left as soon as possible. By morning, I had found a place hidden under bushes where I could sleep. The survival training I had before I came to Vietnam came to mind and guided my actions. In daylight, I got my directions and decided to make for the Hmong area. The food from the other prisoner was a godsend. Later I stole food from gardens or storage areas around houses. Water was a problem except when it rained. Then the malaria got me. That man who found me on the trail, took me home, then to the Catholic mission was a real hero, not afraid of the consequences of helping me."

Jon leaned back and almost instantly fell asleep. Thai and I sat by him and thought about his experiences. Thai was making movements with his hands and arms like they were moving up a wall. I asked what he was doing.

"This is the exercise the therapist told me to do to get more mobility in my shoulder."

We bought plates of rice and vegetables for a late lunch, our one big meal, and ate there on the deck. We still had fruit from Father Stephen, and our money was nearly gone. Jon awoke and ate his plateful with great appetite. The malaria must be letting go again.

The afternoon passed. Jon went to the cabin and slept again. Thai wandered about on deck, sometimes talking to a crew member or other passengers. I sat in the deck chair and watched the shoreline. The countryside had changed. Cultivated fields came up to the riverbank. I saw a water buffalo pulling a cart. A boy sat on the buffalo, playing his bamboo flute. The engine made enough noise that I couldn't hear the flute, though. I dozed some, too.

After sunset, just as the darkness thickened, we came to some rapids and a narrowing of the river. The crew spoke to the passengers on deck. When they came to me, Thai appeared and translated, "Get down. This is where they were shot at on the trip up."

I was down on the deck in a flash, as were Thai and the others. I worried about Jon. He was safe in the cabin, but would he wake up and start walking on the deck?

I started across the deck on my hands and knees.

"What?" Thai said.

"Jon," I said.

"Oh, I stopped by the cabin as I came up. He's awake but will stay where he is until this danger is past."

Zing. A bullet sang overhead. Another, then another. They were coming from both sides of the river now. Everyone was flat on the deck. Only the helmsman was in danger in his high, glassed-in lookout. I prayed for his safety. He was responsible for the safety of all of us on the boat.

It took nearly twenty minutes to get through the narrows. Then we were back in the middle of a quiet stream, farther and farther from the shore. The crew was the first to move around, then all of us, relieved to be out of danger for a while.

"There's one more place where the channel is near the shore on one side of the river. Guerillas can shoot at us there, but that's not until early morning," Thai said. "They aren't trying to stop the riverboat from running, just trying to terrorize the people. Terror is their main tool."

Jon, walking by himself, came out on deck and sat near me. The breeze was cooling now that the sun had gone down. We sat there, not talking, enjoying being together and the pleasant evening.

"Jon, tell me about Bryan. You know who he is or what he is and does. Thai won't tell me anything about him. But you must tell me."

He stirred in his chair. I could tell he didn't want to tell me.

"Well, yes, I know him. I won't tell you the name I know. Why are you so interested in him, Connie?"

"We have something going for us. I don't know what will come of it. Bryan was so nice; we laughed at the same things when we went out in Hong Kong. And I found that we shared the faith. I thought he was Australian then. He was with us when I went to the meeting for you; then on the plane back to Hong Kong, he told me that he had engineered my trip to Dalat. He turns up almost everywhere I go: Okinawa, the hospital in Hong Kong when Thai had the surgery on his shoulder. I'm surprised that he hasn't showed up here."

"Yes, he is a fine man. But his work is demanding and elusive. I don't know much about it myself. But he gets things done. Do you think you should be interested in someone like that? You've never been able to keep secrets or lie about anything in your life. You are like an open book."

"You don't know how I've kept secrets since I started working to get you free. Mom and Dad still don't know about the shooting near Dalat, or about this trip."

Jon grinned at me. He knew I could keep a secret if it meant danger to someone I loved, but it's true that I don't lie well. But I knew him, too. He wasn't going to tell me any more about Bryan.

Chapter Sixteen

We were in our bunks and asleep shortly after dark. I could hear people passing the door, but could see nothing through the louvered door. When I was just dropping off to sleep in the top bunk, I heard Thai come in quietly and stretch out on the floor. I guess he felt we were all safer to be together.

The sharp crack of sniper fire jerked us awake as we neared An Loc early in the morning. My heart pounded like it would jump out of my chest. Bullets hit the boat, but the crew had learned how to avoid them, so no one was hit.

We ate the last of the fruit, two oranges and a mango, from Father Stephen for breakfast. We had slept in our clothes, so morning rituals were simple, washing faces at the tiny lavatory in the cabin and combing short hair. The communal toilet was just beyond the last cabin.

"When we stop at An Loc, I'll go ashore and find a telephone," Thai said. "I'll call the office and have someone meet the boat when we arrive in Saigon. You should go directly to the hospital, Jon."

"I know I'll have to go for a checkup soon. I might as well get it over with," Jon said.

"I'll tell them to make the arrangements, then."

We were at An Loc almost an hour, unloading passengers and freight, then loading more passengers and freight. Thai made his phone call and came back. I watched the activity on the dock and boat. All along this riverfront were warehouses, with men going in and out, some with loads on carts, some carrying smaller articles in two baskets balanced from each end of a pole on the shoulder. The humidity was climbing the nearer we came to the coast.

Jon seemed more alert this morning, and his eyes were clear blue once more.

"It was the color of that fellow's eyes that made me know that the American they rescued wasn't you. His face was so swollen; no one could recognize him. But I knew your eyes were not brown," I told Jon.

Three hours later, we were in the outskirts of Saigon. The boat would stop first at the Cho Lon dock on the south side of the Dong Nai, then proceed down the river and across to the main Saigon dock.

At Cho Lon, we were out on the deck when a US army colonel came running up the gangway as soon as it was set up. Jon and Thai both jumped to their feet and greeted the colonel, a tall, slim man with a long, thin face. A salute wasn't enough for the colonel. He hugged Jon and started to hug Thai, but Thai backed away, so the colonel shook hands with him.

"Connie, this is Colonel Rawlinson, our commander. Colonel, this is my twin sister, Connie Osborne. She's a missionary, a teacher in Hong Kong. She helped find me and bring me back to Saigon."

I shook hands with the colonel and smiled.

"I had begun to believe that I would never see this day," he said. He pulled out his handkerchief and wiped his eyes.

"I think it would be well for you to get off the boat here, Jon," he continued. "We have the car. But Connie, would you go ahead to the Saigon dock? Someone who said his name was Rob will be there to meet you. He's a little annoyed that you did this without him. We'll take Jon directly to the hospital for a checkup, and you can come to the hospital later today. Is that all right?"

"Well, yes," I said, "as long as I can see Jon in the hospital. I'll need to call our parents immediately."

"The best phone connections are in Saigon. Rob will take you to a phone, I'm sure." The colonel began to move Jon and Thai toward the gangway.

Thai took their small bags, and all three walked down to the dock. Jon looked back and waved.

The dock was a hive of activity, men going here and there, some carrying loads, some guiding the crates as they were lowered to the docks, and departing passengers weaving in between.

About half an hour more passed before the riverboat left Cho Lon's dock and headed for Saigon's. I stood by the rail the whole time until we tied up at the Saigon dock. I could see Bryan in sport shirt and khaki pants standing on the dock, tapping his foot with impatience. *He probably is going to be upset with me,* I guessed.

Bryan bounded up the gangway, his eyes searching the deck.

"Where are Jon and Thai?" he demanded.

No greeting, no hug, nothing.

"The colonel met them at the Cho Lon dock and took them in his car to the hospital so Jon could have a checkup. He had malaria again; just now getting over it. But, other than the malaria, I thought he looked pretty good. Thin, though," I rambled on, "and hello to you, too."

He smiled then and gave me a quick hug and a kiss.

"I must get to a phone and call our parents. The colonel said you would take me to some good phone connections."

"All right. Come on, let's go." He took my bag in one hand and my hand in the other and pulled me down the gangway.

My parents were astounded to hear my news. What was I doing in Saigon, they asked. And how did I get to the place where Jon was? And was Jon okay? And on and on.

We were in the Grand Hotel, a very grand place to be dressed in worn, dirty pants and shirt and hiking boots. I looked around at the lobby. My eyes were dazzled at the shining chandeliers and the plush chairs and sofas.

"I want to go on to the hospital now. Thanks for taking me to the phone."

"I just got a room for you here. I thought maybe you would like to clean up. Do you have all you need in the bag?" Bryan asked.

"Oh, well, that would be great. And yes, I have clean clothes and sandals in the bag."

"Here's the key. I have something I need to do. I'll meet you back here at the phone bank in an hour, and then we'll go to see Jon."

Jon looked pale and sickly in the hospital gown. He had looked better in the Catholic clinic. But he was shaved and his hair cut, so he looked more normal.

I looked and felt better, too, since my cleanup at the hotel.

"I feel a little upset with your sister, Jon. How could she and Thai do this rescue without letting me know? I could have helped, I'm sure," Bryan said.

I laughed. "Thai had it all planned out, except for the engine of the jeep quitting. I had the days off for the Moon Festival, so came as soon as Thai cabled. I drove the jeep; that helped. Thai spoke the languages, so we got along okay."

Then I turned to Jon. "What do the doctors say about your condition?"

"I haven't had any tests yet. That'll take a day or two, I think. When do you have to go back to Hong Kong?"

"I have classes on Monday, my language classes, and then the English class I teach. So I have a reservation for Sunday afternoon. This is Saturday. Will they do the tests before I need to leave?"

An older man in a white coat came in the room. He carried a chart in one hand and had a stethoscope around his neck.

"I was just about to start some tests on you, Osborne, but your colonel pulled some strings and you are to leave on the med-evac plane tonight. You are certainly well enough to fly to the States, so good-bye, it's been nice to meet you." He shook Jon's hand and was gone out of the room before any of us could say a thing.

A nurse in khaki traveling gear came into the room. "So, you're going on the med-evac tonight. That leaves at six, about two hours from now, so you will need to get ready now. We have to get you out to Tan Son Nhut and settled on the plane before takeoff. Do you have other clothes? Or bags? I'm sorry," she said to us, "you need to go. The patient will leave shortly."

"Connie, I'm sorry, but it's probably for the best. Thanks for all your help. I love you. You are the greatest sister in the world."

I hugged him once more, and we walked out of Jon's room. In a moment, the nurse appeared, pushing Jon in a wheelchair. We walked to the elevator with them, and then Jon was gone.

"Well, that was quick. I don't feel that I've really talked with Jon. I've just seen him for a few minutes. I feel left out."

"Connie, Jon's right. It's best for him to leave the country immediately. We don't know what the guerillas would do if it were broadcast that he had escaped them, and the details might endanger those who helped him." Bryan had his arm around my shoulders, and we just stood there looking at the closed elevator door.

Bryan asked, "How about something to eat? I can see that you are almost dead on your feet. You've had a hard few days."

"I'm okay. But some good American food would be great. I like rice, but I'm not used to having it for every meal," I said.

We went to a bowling alley. The few tables and chairs just inside the door looked ordinary, but they served the best American-style hamburgers and French fries I had eaten since I left the States. It was wonderful.

Bryan took me back to the Grand. "I have some things to do tonight," he said. "I will pick you up about ten tomorrow morning."

My plane left at three o'clock. We would decide the next morning what we would do.

We ate breakfast in the hotel on Sunday morning, then walked to a nearby park. It was amazing how a few trees and bushes deadened the sound of the horns, motors, and squeals of tires on the street. The quiet was calming, and I felt uplifted by it. Bryan pulled me down on a bench and kept his arm around me as we sat.

"Connie, I want to say something to you. It seems that we just see each other for a few minutes as we are passing by on the way somewhere else. I would like to spend a long time with you, get to know you better. But I don't know when that could be. The situation here in Vietnam is unstable, and probably will heat up even more. I don't know how long I will be here and where I might go next."

"Bryan, I don't know what your job is. Jon says I shouldn't be interested in you, because I don't keep secrets well and I can't tell a lie with a straight face. But I like you and enjoy being with you. Even though I miss you when I don't see you, I will be busy teaching, and I have obligations in the contract, so perhaps we can leave it at that for a while. We'll see each other when we can. Oh, and I liked the letter you wrote me. I could stand a few more of those."

I put my hand on his face, then reached up and kissed him lightly on the mouth.

Bryan smiled, "I could use a few more of those, too." And kissed me hard.

On board the plane to Hong Kong, I leaned back in my seat and dreamed. In time, those dreams came true. I finished my contract, and about that same time Bryan was posted to Washington. There was a quiet wedding in the church of the small town where my parents lived then. A healthy Jon was the best man, and my friend from Hong Kong, Bobbie Jo, was the maid of honor. And life went on.

Baby Merilee

Chapter One

Libby Brown dressed quickly in the examining room, then went into the doctor's office to hear his diagnosis.

"I doubt that you will ever get pregnant, Mrs. Brown. The ruptured appendix that you had when you were in Africa with the Peace Corps caused an infection that left too much scar tissue. But if you should happen to get pregnant, let me know." The doctor smiled as if he were giving a present to her. Perhaps it was the only way he could tell a patient bad news. But to Libby, the words were like a hammer beating on her head as she heard them again and again.

She got in her car and drove through the small town to her home. The forsythia, daffodils, and Bradford pears were in full bloom. But Libby didn't see the beauty of the spring after the cold and dreary winter. Those words, "never get pregnant" continued to echo through her mind. She went into the house through the garage door, put her purse and keys on the counter, and went on into the den. She looked at the comfortable chairs, sat down in her favorite rocker, and heard those words with every rock. She felt numb with shock. It had never occurred to her that they wouldn't have children eventually.

She picked up the morning paper from the stool where Tom had laid it. He always glanced at the headlines before he left for work as an engineer at the clay refining plant, then put it on the stool to finish when he got home. She read the lines with no idea of what she read. But a picture jumped out at her. Someone in town had gone to China to adopt a baby girl and now had returned home with the child in her arms. Libby's arms ached for a baby to hold. She remembered holding babies in Ghana when they were brought to the clinic where she had worked, and how they had loved her and she them. She had thought when she and Tom married that they would soon have a baby. But that seemed unlikely to happen now. Could she go to China and adopt a baby?

By the time Tom got home that afternoon, she had it all worked out in her mind. They could fly to Hong Kong and visit her mother's old friend, Dr. Bobbie Jo Marston, and go on into China from there. She had visited Hong Kong several times with her parents when they lived in Bangkok, and had seen the 169 Boundary house where her mother had lived and studied Cantonese, and the college where she had taught English before she had finished her contract and had married Dad. The family had lived in all parts of the world, and Dad was gone a lot on department business doing something or other, but they knew that he loved them above all else.

"Libby, what did the doctor say?" Tom asked as he stepped into the kitchen from the garage.

She tried to swallow the knot in her throat and reached up in the cabinet for a glass to get some water. She looked at Tom over the top of the glass and saw the worry begin to furrow his forehead.

"I'm okay, but the doctor said I'd probably never get pregnant. That infection after the appendix deal I had in Ghana left lots of scar tissue, and even surgery wouldn't really increase my chances." Tears that had been kept in check all afternoon began to flow now. Tom put his arms around her and murmured his love in her ear.

"You and I make it okay, don't we? And we always will."

Libby remembered how she felt when she met Tom. She had returned to graduate school, and at a church meeting about a construction group building a clinic in Ghana, she had been asked to talk about the country. Afterward, Tom had stopped to talk about some points. That led into other talks, and eventually marriage.

Later, as they ate the meal she had prepared, they were quiet. Finally, she said, "Tom, what do you think about adopting?"

"That's okay, but do you think we could? I have heard that it is a long wait, and since we have moved around a lot, we might have a hard time. We had other things to keep us busy until now."

"Today in the paper I saw a picture of a woman from this area who had gone to China and adopted a baby girl. What would you think about that?"

"Well, I have heard that many baby girls were being abandoned in China because of the one-child law. But I hadn't thought about us doing it. Maybe we could. At least we could investigate it."

The next morning, Libby found the phone number of the woman pictured in the paper and called her. The number was busy. Libby kept calling, and finally after lunch the phone rang. A woman answered, "Yes, I do have a baby girl, but she and I both need to sleep now. Good-bye."

Libby looked at the telephone receiver, then had to laugh.

She laughed again that night as she told Tom about it. "I think I'll just write her a note, and then she can call me when it's convenient for her. I'd probably be tired out with a baby in the house, too."

It took much filling out of forms, FBI background checks, notarized financial statements, letters of recommendation from friends and employers, clearance from the local police departments, physical exams, even tests of their drinking water. And the nearly ten thousand dollars they had spent so far. Then frustrating months and months to work out the details with the adoption agency, but one day the summons came to get tickets to fly to Hong Kong. It was spring again, a time for new life and a new start for their family. Travel to Meichow, where the orphanage was, would be arranged by the agency.

Aunt Bobby Jo met them at the airport in Hong Kong. "How are Connie and Bryan, Libby?"

Libby threw her arms about the doctor. She saw white in the dark hair and wrinkles in the face that had not been there before. Well, Aunt Bobby Jo was a little older than her own mother, so was really past retirement age.

"They're all right," Libby said. "We thought that Dad would be restless, but he seems to really like retirement. They bought a place on the Lake of the Ozarks, not too far from Kansas City and St. Louis, so they can go somewhere or do something when they want a change. Mom is teaching English as a second language to internationals, so she is happy."

They put the bags into the small car that Bobby Jo pointed out, then both Libby and Tom walked to the driver's side of the car.

"Did one of you want to drive?" the doctor asked. They all three laughed at the mistake.

"It takes a while to shift into right-hand-drive cars, you know that," Libby said.

"Yes, I know. And did you know that 169 Boundary is about to be no more?"

"What do you mean?" Libby asked.

"Now that the new airport is actually being built and the height regulation around the old airport soon to be canceled, a development company will tear down the old three-story building and build a twenty- or thirty-story building."

"Where will the mission office move to?" Libby asked.

"They bought space in Mongkok, near the subway stop, so it is more convenient for most people who need to go to our office. But it was heart-wrenching for me to move after all these years. That third-floor flat was home to me, even after it was cut up into two smaller flats," the doctor said.

Libby was too astounded to answer. Tom cleared his throat and said, "Do you have a good place to live now?"

"Oh, yes. It's small and no more high ceilings, but it is comfortable and near to the clinic where I work. It's in Mongkok, too, you remember. There's a car park down under the building, so I have everything I need. That's where we are going now."

The doctor was up and gone when Libby and Tom awoke the next morning, even though she had talked until late, asking about Libby's parents and about Tom and Libby themselves. She had offered good advice about the trip into China and how to tell if the baby was in good health.

Most of the day was gone before Libby and Tom finished arrangements for their trip. They must ride the train to Canton, visit the adoption agency office, then ride the train on to the orphanage in Meichow and return with a baby girl. A child had already been assigned to them, and Libby looked at the picture often. The little face appealed to them, and the number across the chest like a prisoner urged them to hurry to her. Tom and Libby would take the baby to the US Consulate in Canton to obtain a nonquota immigrant visa.

Libby and Tom went first to the China Travel office a couple of blocks from where the doctor lived now. They presented their passports, showed the papers from the agency, and asked for a visa. Libby felt like she was in a dream. Everything was going like clockwork now. There had been no breakdown in the procedures yet.

They watched as the ticket agent, a young woman dressed in a white blouse and black skirt, stamped the visas in their passports. She carried them over to a man sitting at a desk. He read the papers, then signed the visas. He got to his feet, hitched up his pants over his bulging stomach, and walked to the counter.

"You want to adopt Chinese baby, yes?" he said.

"Yes, sir, we do. The agency assured us that all the paperwork was done and there would be no problem," Tom answered.

"No problem with the visa. But some other departments don't like because the adoption department is getting so much money, and they try to make trouble. But your papers are in order, so should be okay."

"What do you mean?" Tom asked.

"Should be no problem," the man said again.

Tom paid for the visas and train tickets. He picked up the passports and other papers, put them in a folder, and then into his pocket. They walked down the crowded sidewalk, looked in shop windows, wrinkled their noses at the smells of molding vegetables, dirt, and urine, and then went down into the MTR entrance. They bought visitors' ticket cards, then went on the platform and caught a train through the under-harbor tunnel to the Hong Kong side. They felt adventurous and a little daring. They had lived in small towns for several years now and had forgotten about big cities and public transportation.

Standing near where they held onto metal poles, two men were talking. A Chinese man was talking English to a British man who talked Cantonese back. They were being polite to each other, but still it seemed odd.

Once on the Hong Kong side, Libby and Tom took a taxi to the American Consulate. They had to wait a short time to see the immigration man, but found that everything was in order. He explained the remarks made by the China Travel agent.

"It is true that we expect a shutdown in the adoptions soon. The fee that the office makes on each adoption is causing jealousy among other offices that have no such lucrative source of income. But it hasn't shut down yet, so you should have no problem."

"I feel like a storm is coming," Libby said when they were out on the sidewalk walking down to the Star Ferry. "Why do they keep saying that we will have no problem?"

Chapter Two

Two days later, Libby and Tom boarded the MTR near Dr. Marston's flat and then changed to the Kowloon-Canton Railway train at Kowloon Tong. For once, they were able to sit down on the train, as the crowd was going into town and they were headed out for Lo Wu on the border. Libby looked out the window after they went through the mountain tunnel into the New Territories. She saw the many tall, slender, high-rise housing estates lining both banks of the river in Sha Tin. They looked like dominoes set on end.

"They look like they would fall over at the slightest push, don't they?" Libby said. "And they have to be built so that they won't fall in a strong typhoon, too." She sometimes felt that she could topple over as easily as dominoes set on end.

"Must be a lot of steel reinforcing that concrete," Tom said.

Would she and Tom have steel in them to keep from toppling over? Where would it come from? She smiled and relaxed. The steel would come from the One who had already sustained them through many frustrating months.

They passed Chinese U. and looked at the sturdy, modern buildings on the hills, then the train went immediately along the shoreline.

"Mom said that when she lived here, a typhoon blew a freighter up on these railroad tracks. It took a big crane to move it back to the deep water."

Soon they were at Lo Wu, following signs to go through Immigration and Customs to leave Hong Kong and to enter China. Then on to the Shen Zhen railroad station just to the left of the KCR stop. There was a long line even this early to get on the Canton train. Once through the gate, they showed the first-class tickets and were escorted to their seats by a young woman in a navy blue uniform. The comfortable gray seats had arms and top backs wrapped with tan slipcovers.

The train moved off slowly and smoothly. Out the windows they could see the factories of Shen Zhen, then the open countryside. Only a few of the green fields were growing crops. Most were left uncultivated. Small houses clustered together into villages, with shrubs marking the field lines. Kapok and firecracker trees were beginning to bloom.

"I guess all the farmers have gone into Shen Zhen to work," Tom said.

An attendant brought a jug of hot tea around. Libby took the glass offered, but Tom asked for a coke. It cost him a dollar US.

Soon the small brick houses along the railroad were closer together and stained with soot, and they realized that the train was coming into Canton. The eighty miles had flown by.

As they walked off the train and into the terminal, they saw a few people standing behind a barrier, waiting to meet someone

"Hey, look, there's a man holding a sign with BROWN on it. Do you think he means us?" Tom asked.

"I don't think Brown is a common name in China. Let's ask him," Libby said.

The man turned out to be from the agency, World Children, that they had been working through. "We thought you might find it hard to locate a taxi and tell him where to go, so I came to meet you." His English was perfect, though he was Chinese. "My name is Matthew Chan."

"Oh, thank you," Libby said. "You've been to school in the United States, I guess."

"Yes, of course. Actually, I'm an ABC. That means American-born Chinese," he laughed. "We will go to the agency office for you to sign some papers, then you are free for a while. A group of three couples and two single women are flying in this afternoon, and I will meet them. Two of the couples and one single woman will go on with you to Meichow and get babies from the same orphanage. The others will go to Wuhan to another orphanage."

They drove to the agency office. The room was plain, but comfortable. Perhaps as a nonprofit organization, they didn't want to spend money on themselves that could be used for their project.

Libby and Tom signed more papers. "We're glad you got here okay. Since you didn't travel with the others, we wondered. But you had friends in Hong Kong to help you get here." The American woman, Mrs. Green, who represented World Children in Canton, had white hair and a wrinkled face. She had a lovely smile that showed her pleasure in seeing babies adopted.

Matt and Mrs. Green took them to a small, nearby restaurant, and ordered a meal in Chinese. Libby and Tom liked Chinese food, but this was better than anything they had eaten in the States. Later they walked through the city market, while Mrs. Green went back to the office and Matt left to meet the others at the airport.

Back at the agency office, Libby and Tom met the group. Mrs. Green told them what to expect from the train and at the orphanage the next day. They ate again and left for the train station. Two China Travel agents met them, both young women, one to accompany each group on their journey.

The distance to Meichow, in northeast Guangtung, made the train trip an overnight one. They followed the agent into a sleeping car. Each set of two seats faced each other. Above each seat, a sleeping shelf was already pulled down, with a small pillow and thin, folded cover on the top end.

Libby and Tom found their seats, and the single woman, Melissa, sat across from them. Their luggage was on the floor between the seats. Libby and Tom were glad they had left their large bags with Dr. Marston in Hong Kong, since Melissa's one big bag took almost all the floor space.

Libby found that the car's one rest room served all and was back quickly. She told Melissa about it saying, "You can't miss it because it smells out in the narrow hallway. There is no commode, just a hole in the floor, with footholds on each side so that you won't slip when you squat." Libby had seen such arrangements before so wasn't surprised, but had heard Melissa say it was her first trip out of the country.

They took off their shoes and laid down, Tom on the top shelf above Libby, and Melissa across from her. The click, clack of the wheels was loud at first, but soon lulled them to sleep. Libby heard first Tom, then

Melissa begin snoring. She thanked God that the long months of filling out forms, submitting documents, and waiting were over. She asked Him to help them to bond with their new daughter and to know how to care for an eight-month-old. Then she, too, was asleep.

"Time to wake up," the China Travel agent called. "We are nearly at Meichow."

Melissa was up instantly, looking through her luggage for something. Tom leaned over his shelf, then slid down to Libby's.

"Morning," he said as he kissed her lightly on the lips. "This is the day we see Merilee for the first time."

"Oh, yes, Lord, make it a good day."

The train stopped before they had their shoes on and the small bags zipped up. They grabbed up everything, helped Melissa with her big bag, and got off the train.

"I haven't even combed my hair," Libby said to the others on the platform.

"The bus is here. We will go to a hotel first, so you can wash and eat breakfast, then we will go out to the orphanage," the China Travel agent said.

The sun was struggling to shine through thin clouds, and the wind whistled across the platform. They pulled their collars up around their necks and hugged themselves to try to warm up.

"I'm so glad that China lets single people adopt," Melissa said. "At home, single people can adopt, but they must compete with couples for what children are available. I'm forty-five, so most agencies consider me too old. But China knows that single people, even up to fifty, make good parents."

Libby hadn't thought about singles wanting to adopt. She only knew the difficulty that couples had. She had thought that she was more excited than anyone was, but she realized that Melissa, and the others, might have the tight, curling muscle in their stomachs, too.

They went to a new, modern hotel, where they showered and changed clothes. The rooms were clean, the beds felt comfortable, and the bathrooms had hot water. Libby thought they could have been in that motel where she and Tom spent the first night of their honeymoon, instead of in the northeast corner of Guangtung Province in China.

While eating the continental breakfast in the side lobby of the hotel, they saw rain begin to fall. The China Travel agent came into the lobby with a wet umbrella.

"There is some mechanical trouble with the bus. We will wait here for it to be fixed."

"About how long will it take to fix it?" one of the men asked.

"Why couldn't this happen when we already had the babies?" one of the ladies said.

"Why not have some tea while we wait?" the agent said, picking up the pot and offering some to Libby.

"Okay, I'll take some," she said. She sighed: problems had begun already.

Chapter Three

Libby and Tom were on the front seat of the bus two hours later. The late spring sun shone on the budding trees. During the thirty-minute ride to the orphanage, Libby saw excitement on Tom's face and felt the tremors in her own stomach.

"Do I look as excited and nervous as I feel?" she asked Tom. "Your face is full of anticipation."

"I do feel happy that we are soon to see our baby. I hope that she is healthy. Do you think she will adjust to us quickly?"

"I hope so. What if she cries all the time? How will we manage on the trip back to Canton? At least now we know it will be on an airplane, not the long trip on the train with Melissa's big suitcase taking up the floor space."

The excited buzz on the bus got louder as other expectant parents worried aloud about the babies awaiting them.

The orphanage sat on a small rise outside of town. The building was a two-story concrete block structure, with bright green fenced yards on each side. Some swings and slides were in one yard. Older children and some adults were coming out of the door to the play yard, now that the rain had stopped. Libby saw that some limped, and others had malformed arms. She realized these older ones were mildly handicapped. She remembered that one couple had said they were offered a boy, but he was handicapped. So the not-perfect ones were abandoned, too.

"Wait here a moment," the China Travel agent said as she stepped out of the bus.

She went into the building and returned with a woman in a white uniform.

"You are so late, we have put the babies down for morning nap. Better you wait for waking up, maybe one hour, then come back," the nurse said.

A groan echoed through the bus. "They are tormenting us," the woman seated behind Libby and Tom said. "But I guess that they don't want to give us an unhappy baby first time we see her."

"This is what we will do," the China Travel agent said over the loudspeaker. "We will do some sightseeing near here, for an hour or so, then return to the orphanage to see your babies."

The bus started up, and they were off to see the sights of Meichow.

"Some of you have asked about a Christian church, since tomorrow is Sunday. We will drive past it, near your hotel, but we won't stop. This is not Sunday; no one will be there." The agent went on, "Tomorrow afternoon, we will drive to the Hakka round houses, spent the night, then return to Meichow on Monday for your meeting with the local officials. Are you happy with that plan?"

They grumbled to themselves. Libby got out the picture of Merilee that World Children had sent to them. Was she a real child, or was it all a make-believe dream? The Chinese name was a made-up name for paperwork, they said, and the real identification was the number across the bottom of the picture. She looked like a prisoner with that number, a chubby baby with apple cheeks and hair standing straight up on her head. Would she ever have that baby in her arms? She looked at Tom. His face was solemn, and a hint of a tear showed in his eyes. He was as disappointed as she was.

The bus drove back into town and down the street from the hotel, past the Catholic, then the Protestant church, through the main business district, with shops open to the street, and past the city hall. The agent talked all the time, telling about the modern buildings they saw. Then they started back to the orphanage.

Libby and Tom and the other prospective parents hopped off the bus and hurried to the door of the orphanage. They were ushered into a reception room filled with green plastic-covered chairs and couches. Almost immediately, a group of caretakers filed in with babies in their arms. Most of the babies were quiet, except one who squalled at the top of her lungs.

Libby looked carefully at the crying baby. Surely that was Merilee. New parents' names were called, and a baby was handed to each. Libby heard their name called, and the crying baby was handed to her.

She felt the hot, little body as she laid Merilee against her shoulder, patting the heaving back. The baby continued to cry. Libby looked at the caretakers and saw that they had tears falling down their cheeks. The one who had carried Merilee held out her hands to take the baby again. But Libby turned away and walked to the window. Merilee's cries grew softer.

"You can have another baby, if you wish. This one cries at lot," the head woman said.

"No, no. This is our baby. We will keep her," Libby said.

Tom took Merilee on his shoulder, and walking, began to sing quietly. The rumble in his chest seemed to fascinate Merilee. She quieted as she looked at Tom.

The caretakers distributed bottles of milk to the parents, and soon the room was full of slurping sounds as the babies drank. Libby's heart was full as she looked at Merilee in Tom's arms. Why would anyone think that she would want another baby just because she cried? This was her child, now and forever.

Merilee saw her caretaker walk past and put her arms up to go to her. When Libby turned away, Merilee cried out. "Not yet, baby. You stay with me for a little longer."

The hour passed too quickly. The babies were tired, and the caretakers took them away to their beds. The new parents went to the bus, some bubbling, some quiet, all with full hearts.

They returned to the hotel for a late lunch, then had free time. Libby and Tom walked around the city center, looked at the shops that sold baby things, admired other babies in strollers or carriers, and found smiles on almost everyone's face. They were recognized as the Americans who were adopting Chinese baby girls.

Sunday morning they walked to church, and found it full, with people standing outside. They were directed to a back-row seat where earphones were hooked up. An English translation for visitors came through. A person sitting nearby explained in good English that this church had been open continuously since it was started in the 1920s. Other churches had been closed, and now all Protestants in the city worshipped here.

After lunch at the hotel, Libby and Tom got on the bus with the other new parents to see the Hakka round houses.

"Why couldn't they be at the orphanage with the babies?" Libby asked herself, then aloud to Tom.

"I guess the visit was arranged this way because we have to see the babies before they are adopted in order to get a nonquota visa. You remember the agency people told us that," Tom said.

The road was full of potholes, and the bus crept along. The fields were greening with crops. The agent began to talk about the three-story structure they were to see, built of pounded dirt and with no windows until the second floor. Hakkas are Chinese, but speak a different dialect from the Cantonese-speaking people in the surrounding area. So for defense, houses were built this way. Inside the circular building was a courtyard and windows that faced it. This must have been a dangerous place for outsiders to live until recent years; the defenses were still in good order.

By this time, most of the new parents were getting tired of rice and vegetables at every meal. So for the evening meal, Tom tried one of the few items on the menu that sounded like American food, a hamburger. It came with a sunny-side up egg on top of it and no bun. But he did get Coca-Cola to drink instead of hot tea.

The next morning, a bright, clear day, the group saw some other landmarks, but Libby, at least, was eager to return to Meichow and the orphanage. The bus pulled into the orphanage grounds in early afternoon, now a very warm day. They were shown into the reception room again. There was a formality to the proceedings now, as three Chinese officials entered with caretakers holding the babies.

Finally, "Mr. and Mrs. Brown," the official said, "please take your baby," and they were handed Merilee. Other names and other babies were handed over. Babies cried, and tears ran down the faces of caretakers and new parents alike. Libby held Merilee, then felt a dampness spreading over the baby and herself. The caretaker saw the situation and took Merilee for a quick change.

Half an hour later, when a little calm had been restored, one of the officials read the adoption contract: the Americans would not rear their girls to be servants, nor would they abandon them, transfer them to other parents, or force them into arranged marriages. They agreed to care for the babies lovingly and grant them inheritance rights, teach them about their heritage, and, if possible, bring them back to visit their homeland.

Then each couple, or single mother, presented the orphanage with a donation of $3000.US, an amount that had been agreed on prior to the ceremony.

Libby and Tom sat down on one of the sofas and began changing Merilee into clothes they had brought. She was wearing a paper towel for a diaper, and the plastic pants were held up by a rubber band. Libby opened the bag they had brought and found a disposable diaper and the clothes to outfit Merilee. Once out of the layers of sweaters and undershirts, with a lacy, embroidered dress on the outside, Merilee was more comfortable and smiled. She was a sturdy eight-month-old, with no physical defects. Libby thanked God for the gift of Merilee and asked for guidance for the future.

Libby joined in the laughter mingled with the tears in that room. Fathers, Tom included, were videoing or snapping pictures, while mothers dressed their new daughters in the clothes purchased with that baby in mind.

Another official began to speak. The room quieted, and then they were asked to sign some more paperwork. The third official, who was a doctor, talked about the condition of the babies, and each parent was given a sheet of paper with the medical history and shot record of their baby. The director of the orphanage spoke to the group and gave gifts of milk powder and medicine for each baby. Libby took the bottle of medicine for Merilee, something for upset stomach, it said in English.

Next, the necessary paperwork for each child was presented. Libby checked for passport, adoption decree, abandonment certificate, and such. They were in both Chinese and English and tied together with a red ribbon.

"Thank you for giving this opportunity to the girls for a better life. Thank you for the donation to the Social Welfare Center," the director said. "Please follow me to the luncheon we have arranged for you."

"I want to carry Merilee. You've held her all morning," Tom said.

Libby gathered up all the papers, bags, and other things they had brought for Merilee. They followed the group into the small dining room, which had cribs for the babies squeezed in. Libby couldn't eat, and she noticed that Tom only picked at the food.

Later, they took Merilee and walked around the orphanage, seeing other girls in their cribs, thirty or forty of them, waiting for the adoption mill to find homes for them.

Back on the bus, with Merilee in Tom's lap, Libby felt that the long wait was over: they finally had their child. But they still were in China, and were a long way from home. They still had to return to Canton, take the baby to an approved doctor for a physical exam, and have an interview with the immigration official at the American Consulate, then wait for the visa to be issued before they could start the journey out of China to the United States.

Chapter Four

"Hey, what's the trouble here?" Tom asked. The bus had not driven a mile from the orphanage when Merilee threw up all over Tom.

Libby took the baby and wiped her mouth and the front of her outfit. The smell threatened to make Libby herself throw up. Tom opened the window, and the fresh air soon revived Libby. "Maybe the baby gets motion sick," she said.

At the hotel, Libby ran water in the bathtub and sat Merilee in it. The baby loved the water, splashing and laughing. Libby, kneeling by the tub, watched and laughed herself.

"This paper says Merilee has had stomach upset problems a lot. I guess that's why they gave us that bottle of medicine." Tom was looking at the papers the doctor at the orphanage had given them.

Later they went downstairs to eat. The hotel had high chairs ready. The waitresses held and played with the babies every free minute they had as they served the new parents. Libby was glad to have a chance to eat some noodles and vegetables.

After the meal, Libby and Tom and the baby walked around outside the hotel. A street market was on a side street. As they walked through the market stalls, many people smiled at and patted the baby. Libby thought the women especially were happy to see this baby girl going into a good home. One older woman had a hostile look in her eyes, but she didn't say anything. Libby wondered if her granddaughter had been abandoned and foreigners had adopted her.

Merilee went to sleep on the walk, and the new family headed back to the hotel. In their room, they found a crib had been moved in, and Tom put the baby down in it. Libby had a bottle ready when the baby awoke about an hour later. She took it right down, and Tom burped her. Soon she was asleep again and slept through the rest of the night.

At breakfast the next morning, Libby and Tom heard stories about the night from the rest of the new parents and laughed with them. One baby had cried most of the night; another had awakened happy three times during the night. Libby saw another group of foreigners come into the hotel dining room. She learned later that it was a group of ten couples from Sweden, there to adopt babies from the same orphanage.

The morning was free. The schedule showed the plane to Canton leaving at 3:00 p.m. Libby and Tom took the baby to a nearby department store that had a handwritten sign in English outside the door saying, "Baby things here." The people in the store were as pleased to see them with a Chinese baby as were the people in the open market the day before. Libby bought a baby carrier to carry Merilee in. The salesladies helped her put it on and put the baby in it. By the time they were back at the hotel, Libby was glad to take it off. Eighteen pounds on her back was heavy!

After a rest and lunch, the new parents gathered at the lobby to go to the airport. The Swedes watched and congratulated them on the babies. They seemed impatient to get their own babies.

On the plane, 150 people filled every seat, along with several babies in laps. Libby, holding Merilee, was glad that the flight was only forty minutes. She thought of the all-night train ride and Melissa's big suitcase, and was thankful. In the airport, Libby saw Melissa carrying her baby in a sling and pulling her big bag along behind her. She thought, *Melissa knows how to manage by herself.* Libby felt relieved that neither they nor anyone else had to help Melissa now when they all had their hands full.

Merilee cried during the flight; probably her ears hurt with the change of air pressure. Libby gave her a small bottle of water, and swallowing helped the baby's ears. As they walked down the steps after the plane landed, they were met with a hot, humid blast. The sun in the western sky still scorched.

Soon they were in an air-conditioned van going to the White Swan Hotel. They found the hotel to be next door to the US Consulate on Shamian Island in downtown Canton. The guide on the bus told them that this was the location of the European merchants when Canton was opened to foreign trading in 1800. One man in the group started asking questions. *He must be a history buff,* Libby thought and stopped listening. She looked at Tom holding a now-sleeping baby and thought the sight wonderful. He had a soft, wondering look on his face that Libby hadn't seen before.

The luxurious White Swan Hotel had adjusted to the recent flood of new parents and babies. There were cribs in each room, and along with the usual soap, shampoo, disposable razor, and toothbrush, they supplied baby soap, shampoo, and powder.

Libby settled the baby in her crib, while Tom found CNN on the TV fascinating.

"Seems like we've been out of the world for several days, so much has happened. Can you see the screen?" Tom asked.

"Yes, but I can't stop watching this baby sleep."

Merilee got them up early the next morning, crying. She was hot and turned her head away from the bottle.

"You have to be well this morning, Merilee. The clinic must say you are well, so we can get your visa for America. Don't be sick." Libby felt frantic.

The fog was thick outside, swirling about their fourth-floor window. Maybe they were in a low-flying cloud. After a quick breakfast, they left immediately for the clinic about a half mile from the hotel, walking through the fog. They could see the sidewalk, but only heard the cars and bicycles on the street.

Libby saw that the clinic was clean, but sparsely furnished. The nurses were friendly and held Merilee carefully as they took her temperature. When they saw the doctor, he said the baby had a bit of a virus, nothing serious, and gave them some medicine for her. He checked her weight and did an EKG. "But I can't sign the papers that the baby is a healthy girl until her fever is gone," he added.

Some of the new parents had appointments that afternoon at the consulate for the visa interview. "I'm glad our appointment is tomorrow, since Merilee has the virus," Libby said.

They went back to their hotel, gave the baby the medicine, and put her down to sleep. Tom went out to walk around, now that the fog was lifting. Libby lay down on the bed and dozed for a while.

They found the baby's temperature normal on Thursday morning, so they hurried to the clinic but had to wait to see the doctor. Libby frowned, then said, "I hate this waiting. If we don't make the visa interview time, we won't get the visa today and will have to wait until a later plane."

She saw the young doctor talking with the other new parents. She prayed that he would be patient, but quick, when their turn came. She looked around at the plain, white walls and brown linoleum floor. Everything was clean, but nothing ornamental. It reminded her of the clinic where she had worked as a pharmacy helper in Ghana. She saw herself putting pills in old, unused church offering envelopes that people had sent from the States. Then she remembered the ruptured appendix and the pain, and the weakness that followed the long illness.

"Hey, where are you going?" Tom said to Merilee, as she struggled to get out of his arms and down on the floor. Another new mother had spread a large towel on the floor and put her baby down to enjoy it. Merilee wanted to be down there. Tom set her down, and she began to make happy noises and crawl around.

Libby laughed at the two little girls, and then a third joined them. They laughed, crowed, and fought over the few toys. The others left as their daughters were examined. Still Libby and Tom waited, while other people saw the doctor. Finally, their name was called, and they entered the exam room.

"I'm glad to see you back so soon. Is the baby over the virus?" the doctor asked.

"She doesn't have fever today, I think, so I guess she is over the virus," Libby said.

The doctor examined Merilee again, and then signed the certificate of good health that the American consulate required.

They paid the fee, left the office, and walked next door to the consulate. A new building, painted so white that it almost blinded a person in the bright sun, it had been built after 1982, when China and the United States reestablished relations. They found a long line going from outside the back door of the building into the visa office—young people, whole families, old people. They walked up the line and found an American marine guarding the door.

"We need to apply for a nonquota immigrant visa. We missed our appointment this morning because the baby was sick. Could we make another appointment?" Tom asked.

"Just a minute." The marine opened the door and talked to someone just inside. A woman stepped out. "You missed your appointment this morning? I'm sorry, but I think there are no more today. Let me ask first, though." She disappeared back into the room and was gone several minutes. When she returned, she was smiling. "You can have the interview late this afternoon, about three thirty. But we can't get the visa to you until tomorrow morning. Yes, that is Saturday, but we work half days on Saturday."

"Fine, we'll be here at three thirty this afternoon," Libby said, then turned to Tom and said, "But that means we'll miss the plane in the morning. It goes at eight thirty."

Chapter Five

Libby and Tom found the interview to be informal and easy. The immigration official, a balding, fortyish, relaxed man, talked like an old friend. "Why did you want to adopt a Chinese baby?" he asked.

"Because we wanted a child and knew this child needed a home," Libby answered.

He kept Merilee's Chinese passport, gave them a receipt, and said, "The visa will be stamped in the passport and brought to your hotel tomorrow morning. Sorry, it won't be early enough for you to make the flight, but you can work that out, can't you?"

Back at the hotel, Libby put Merilee in her crib and picked up the phone. "I'll call Aunt Bobby Jo so she won't meet the plane in the morning. The flight is only twenty-five minutes, and the drive from Mongkok to the airport takes at least that long."

When she hung up, she turned to Tom. "Aunt Bobbie Jo suggested that we take the bus. A through bus leaves from one of the hotels about four Saturday afternoon. She thinks it might be from this hotel, but we could ask at the front desk and they would probably know where it goes from. She's ridden that bus and says it is an air-conditioned, comfortable bus, and seats are reserved. No one is allowed to stand."

Tom hurried down to the lobby and inquired at the front desk and was referred to another desk. "Yes, a bus goes from here every afternoon at four and arrives at Kowloon Tong station in Hong Kong about six, then at the Peninsula Hotel about six-thirty. I can make reservations for you now," a young woman in the regulation white blouse and dark skirt said.

Back in their room, Libby smiled at the news and said, "Aunt Bobbie Jo said she would wait at the clinic or at home for us to call her whenever we get to the Kowloon Tong Station. But my mind is relieved that it's all arranged."

When the passport with visa arrived the next morning, Tom and Libby felt released in a way and decided to do some sightseeing. They hired an English-speaking guide and drove to the park, where a statue of fighting goats depicted the local mythology about the creation of the world. The home of Sun Yat Sen, in the same park, was interesting, as was the guide's information about the beginnings of the 1911 revolution in Canton.

Back at the hotel with a sleeping baby, they ordered a lunch sandwich from room service. Libby repacked the suitcases, and Tom went ahead to check out. The hotel had cheerfully agreed to a late checkout since they had been delayed in leaving.

They boarded the bus soon after it drove up in front of the hotel, but found a Chinese man settled in their assigned seats. "Just take any seat," he said, "we don't go by reservation when the bus is not full." The only row of two seats now empty was the one behind their own reserved ones, so they sat there. Then Libby said quietly to Tom, "I know why he wanted our seats. This one is over the wheel. But my legs are short, so I don't mind."

Merilee enjoyed the bus, poking fingers in every cranny of the seat. She struggled to get off of Tom's lap to investigate the floor, but Libby distracted her by showing her cars and trucks out the window. The baby seemed not to know the difference in the people caring for her and didn't cry much, as long as she got her bottles of milk. She thrived on the attention of two doting parents.

Libby realized the scene out the window was different from the train's viewpoint that they had seen several days before. The superhighway went through the main street of the city, past gardens and parks and at times under a canopy of tall trees. Homes seemed to be set back away from the street and couldn't be seen from the bus.

Outside the city, the road went past green fields, with only a few trees, and small villages of brick or unpainted wooden houses with tiled roofs. The absence of trees reminded Libby that she had heard that all trees in Hong Kong had been used during the Japanese war for cooking fuel; perhaps the same was true here. Large factories with dormitories for workers were here and there in the landscape. The factories became more numerous as the bus neared Shen Zhen, a special economic zone.

The bus stopped at the immigration gates of Shen Zhen, and all the passengers got off to walk into a large, barnlike building. Libby and Tom were at the end of one line, the only foreigners, but a second line opened when another bus pulled into the parking lot. The man second in front of them had some difficulty, and finally was escorted out of the line to a nearby office. Tom pulled on Libby's arm, and they moved over to be first in the new line.

"You adopt Chinese baby girl?" the man at the desk asked. He smiled and patted Merilee on the hand, then quickly checked their passports and Merilee's visa and passed them on through. They walked out the door ahead and found their bus waiting for them there.

Shen Zhen was built up with factories on both sides of the road, showing familiar names on the signs, Motorola, Sony, Philips, and Hoover among others. "I read that this city has boomed to almost three million in just the last fifteen years," Tom said. "I can see why it has grown so fast; all the factories are moving out of Hong Kong and into China for cheaper wages and more room to expand."

In less than a half hour, they were at the border with Hong Kong, and there was another immigration line to go through. Some of their fellow passengers were first in line, and once again they were the only foreigners and were at the end of the line. When a second line opened, Tom stepped over into it, but Libby stayed where she was. She was the next in line, so why move? However, the immigration man shook his head as he questioned the man in front of Libby. There was more talk. Libby looked around and saw that Tom was already through the other line, waiting for her at the door. She wished that she had followed Tom when he moved.

A woman in the immigration uniform came to the desk, then escorted the man in front to an office nearby. Libby wondered if this was an activist trying to escape from China. Or maybe he had someone else's passport or a fake visa. What was the trouble?

The bus driver came to the door, looking for them. Libby waved to the driver and Tom, then presented her and the baby's documents to be looked at. They were through the formalities a moment later, and on out to the bus.

The light was fading as they entered Hong Kong's New Territories and drove through the sunset as they went from one country city to another.

They looked at the towering housing estates in Sha Tin from a new angle as they approached the Lion Rock Mountain tunnel. They still looked like dominoes, ready to fall. But Libby realized that with God's help, she had shown her steel and ability to cope.

On the other side of the tunnel, Libby looked with interest at the university where her mother had taught years before, and then the bus pulled up at the Kowloon Tong Station.

Libby called the doctor's cell phone, and she was soon there to pick them up. "Let me see that baby," she said as she put the car in "park" and reached out her arms. Tom put their bags in the small trunk and crawled into the backseat. Libby got in front and held her arms out to the baby.

"No, no. I don't have a baby seat, so she must go in the backseat," the doctor said as she lifted Merilee over to Tom.

It was a happy evening as they showed off the baby, putting her down on the floor on a big towel where she tried to crawl. Aunt Bobbie Jo played with her in the process of examining her. Tom retrieved the sheet of medical information from the folder of papers, and the doctor nodded her head. "She's had her shots, and maybe measles; it's not clear whether she had the measles or had the immunization for measles," she said as she read the paper.

They talked about what to feed Merilee besides the eight bottles of reconstituted dry, skim milk. "She's had some applesauce, but that seems to be all," the doctor said. "I believe she could have some cereal and pureed vegetables. Take her to a pediatrician as soon as you get home, and he'll tell you what she needs. I don't think you want to start her on anything more that is new to her while you are still traveling. About the upset stomachs, probably they gave her some food or seasoning that disagreed with her. You will find what it was in a few days by observing her."

On Sunday, Libby went to church with the older woman, back to the flat to get Tom and the baby, and then to an English restaurant for lunch. Both Tom and Libby were glad to have something other than Chinese food.

"When do you plan to retire, Aunt Bobbie Jo?" Libby asked. "You have had long years of service here, but isn't it time to go home?" She knew the doctor was older than her own mother was, and she knew how old her mother was. She saw again the salt and pepper hair and the wrinkles that disappeared in smiles. "Where will you live back in the States?"

"Oh, I will live in Virginia, probably on the farm where I grew up. Some of my brothers have built houses there, and I would like to be near them. But they have full lives, and since our parents are gone, I haven't been in a hurry to retire." She looked down at her plate.

Libby thought, *she hates to leave this place where she has lived and worked for all these years. And when she goes home, she won't have much to keep her busy.*

After lunch, they drove to Boundary Street. Tom stayed in the car with the sleeping baby in his lap, but Libby and Bobbie Jo got out and peered through the gate of iron bars at the 167-169 building. "They won't start tearing it down until the new airport actually opens, and that has been delayed twice already. No one knows when it will be finished."

Libby looked at a small section of the stucco-covered walls, once cream-colored, but now stained by years of dirt and mold. She remembered that when her mother lived here, the mission had leased the building, but about 1970, they had bought the whole structure and named it "Richmond Building." She traced the name on a brass plaque on the wall beside the gate.

The afternoon and evening were spent resting, using the doctor's washer and dryer, and once again repacking, leaving out comfortable clothes to wear on the plane on Monday. The baby started diarrhea, and Libby was thankful for disposable diapers. How would she manage on the plane? Bobbie Jo found some medicine that the baby could take that slowed it down some, but Merilee already had a rash from it. *I'll be glad to get home,* Libby thought.

They were at the airport early, sailed through Immigration, and boarded the plane. When they took off, Libby looked back at the region that would soon return to China's sovereignty. She breathed a big sigh of relief. She was glad she had come to China, even with all the expenses, because she was going home with her new daughter. She knew that the future might not be easy, as all parents faced with a baby, but she and Tom would face whatever came together, with the same God-given strength that supported them during this time.